THE 45% HANGOVER

Stuart MacBride is the No.1 bestselling author of the DS Logan McRae series and the Ash Henderson novels.

His novels have won him the CWA Dagger in the Library, the Barry Award for Best Debut Novel, and Best Breakthrough Author at the ITV3 Crime Thriller awards. In 2012 Stuart was inducted into the ITV3 Crime Thriller Hall of Fame. He was crowned World Stovies Champion 2014.

He lives in the north-east of Scotland with his wife, Fiona, and cat, Grendel.

For more information visit StuartMacBride.com

By Stuart MacBride

The Logan McRae Novels
Cold Granite
Dying Light
Broken Skin
Flesh House
Blind Eye
Dark Blood
Shatter the Bones
Close to the Bone
The Missing and the Dead

The Ash Henderson Novels
Birthdays for the Dead
A Song for the Dying

Other Works
Sawbones (a novella)
12 Days of Winter (short stories)
Partners in Crime (Two Logan and Steel short stories)
The Completely Wholesome Adventures of Skeleton Bob
The 45% Hangover (A Logan and Steel novella)

Writing as Stuart B. MacBride
Halfhead

Stuart MacBride

THE 45% HANGOVER

HARPER

Harper
An imprint of HarperCollinsPublishers
77–85 Fulham Palace Road
Hammersmith
London W6 8JB

www.harpercollins.co.uk

This paperback edition 2014
1

First published by HarperCollinsPublishers 2014
Copyright © Stuart MacBride 2014
Stuart MacBride asserts the moral right to be identified as the author of this work

The Missing and the Dead extract © Stuart MacBride 2014
Cover layout design © HarperCollins*Publishers* 2014
Cover photographs © Jorg Greuel/Getty Images

A catalogue record for this book is available from the British Library

ISBN: 978-0-00-812826-5

Typeset in Meridien 10.25/13.5 pt by
Palimpsest Book Production Limited, Falkirk, Stirlingshire

MIX
Paper from
responsible sources
FSC™ C007454
FSC
www.fsc.org

Friday 19th September

(The Day After)

Prologue

'GAAAAAAAAAAAAAAAAAAAAAAAAAAAAAGH!' The scream cut through the world like a rusty chainsaw.

It reverberated back from the walls, jerking Logan fully awake. Then making him wish he wasn't. Something large and spiky was loose inside his head, scrabbling at the back of his eyes with long dirty claws. He screwed his eyes shut and lay there, till the echoes faded.

'WHAT THE HELL DID YOU DO?'

He gritted his teeth and opened one eye. Then the other one. Wide. Then his mouth.

Oh dear Jesus, no...

They were lying in bed. No idea *whose* bed, but it was definitely a bed – metal framed, with a brass headboard. Floral-print duvet.

Him and Detective Chief Inspector Steel. In bed. Together.

Her hair was flat on one side, poking out in all directions on the other, her lined face pulled into a shape of utter disgust. Worse yet, it didn't look as if she was wearing a top.

No, no, no, no...

One arm wouldn't move, but he used the other one to grab the duvet and pull it up to his chin. 'Why are we—'

3

'IF YOU SO MUCH AS—'

'STOP BLOODY SHOUTING!' He screwed his eyes shut, teeth gritted. Every heartbeat made the spiky thing in his skull throb. *'Please.'*

'I'll shout if I want to! You try waking up naked, in bed, with a sodding *man* and see how you like it.'

'Naked?' Oh no, not this ... He raised the edge of the duvet an inch.

'If you so much as peek, I swear to God, Laz, I'll rip your bits off and give them back to you as a suppository!' She hit him. 'Get out.'

'Arm's gone to sleep.'

She kicked him under the duvet.

'Ow!'

'Get out!'

'I can't.' His right leg wouldn't move either. He jerked it to the side, but it barely moved, something was keeping it where it was. Something solid. 'Oh *no.*'

She glared at him. 'You bloody men are all the same aren't you? Sex, sex, sex. Well let me tell you something, you randy wee shite, if you ever breathe a *word* of this to anyone, I'm going to...' The glare turned into a frown. 'Why can't I move my arm?'

Then her head turned. She reached up with her other hand and pulled the pillow to one side.

Logan's left hand, and her right, poked between the bars of the headboard, fixed there by a set of police-issue handcuffs.

When he shifted his other foot, the duvet rode up just enough to show the handcuff holding his right ankle to the bars at the other end.

Steel slumped back against her pillow. 'Oh God... Because naked wasn't bad enough, it had to be *kinky*!' She covered her mouth with a hand. 'I'm going to be sick.'

4

'Thank you very much. How do you think *I* feel?' He ran a hand across his forehead, then squeezed at the temples. Maybe, if he squeezed hard enough, the headache would vanish? Or his head would explode. Right now either was preferable to this.

'How much did I *drink* last night?'

Good question.

Thursday 18th September

(Referendum Day)

1

The rumpled lump in the wrinkled suit raised an eyebrow, then pulled the fake cigarette from her mouth. 'What time do you call this?'

Logan hung his jacket on the hook behind the door, then checked his watch – nine thirty. 'Half an hour before my shift starts.' He crossed to the window and lowered the blind, shutting out the darkness. 'Now get out of my seat.'

'You see the latest polls? We're going to do it, can feel it in my water.' Steel wriggled her bum further into his office chair, both feet up on his desk. 'Tell you, it's a momentous day, Laz. Mo-sodding-mentous.' From the look of her hair, she'd celebrated by dragging herself through a hedge, sideways.

'Seat.' He hoiked a thumb at the door. 'Some of us have work to do.'

'Course I gave my team a rousing speech when they came on, this afternoon. "Ask not what your country can do for you..."'

'You're not allowed to campaign on Police Scotland property.'

A frown. 'Since when?'

'There's been like, a dozen memos.' Logan unlocked the

filing cabinet and hauled out the thick manila folder sitting at the front of the top drawer. 'Now, would you *please* sod off and let me get on with it?'

Steel raised her feet from the desk and pushed off, setting the chair spinning with her still in it. Lowered her feet down onto the windowsill instead. 'This time tomorrow we'll have risen up to be the nation again...' Then she launched into a gravelly version of 'Flower of Scotland', getting all wobbly on the long notes, and battering out the optional Tourette's bits.

No point fighting with her – it'd only make it worse.

Logan dumped the folder on the desk and sank into one of his visitors' chairs. Pulled the desk phone over and punched in DC Stone's number. Listened to it ring.

A knock on the office door, and Detective Sergeant Rennie poked his head into the room. 'Sorry, Guv, but any chance you can keep the singing down a bit? Only people are complaining.'

Steel paused, mid-warble. 'Unpatriotic sods.' Then started up again.

Rennie nodded, setting his floppy blond quiff wobbling. 'Yeah, but the mortuary says the dead are crawling out the fridge drawers and hacking off their ears.' A grin. Then he ducked out again just before the stapler battered against the door where he'd been.

If anything, Steel had got louder.

On the other end of the phone, Detective Constable Stone picked up. *'Guv? You forcing bagpipes up a cat's bum in there?'*

Logan put a finger in his other ear. 'Stoney: where are we with Chris Browning?'

'Give us a chance, shift hasn't even started yet. Still waiting for the computer to boot up.'

'Soon as it does, get onto uniform – I want an update on my desk by five past ten. Then we're doing the briefing. And tell Wheezy Doug he's on teas.'

'*Guv.*'

Steel got to the big finale, and finished with her arms outstretched and head thrown back, as if she'd just finished running a marathon. Making hissing noises to mimic her own applause. 'Thank you, Aberdeen, I love you.' Then let her arms fall at her side. Pursed her lips. And had a scratch. 'Pffff... What do you think, landslide?'

Logan clicked the handset back into its cradle. 'Don't you have a murder or something to solve?'

'Did it yesterday, while you were off. Had a cake to celebrate and everything.' She creaked his chair left, then right again. 'Bit quiet today, to be honest. I've got a Major Investigation Team with nothing major to investigate. Going to have to drag something out of the cold-case file if we're not careful.'

'Then go do something about that guy from Edinburgh who got the crap beaten out of him.'

'Not major enough.' She waved a hand. 'And the scumbag was a drug dealer. Probably deserved it. If they'd *killed* him, it'd be a different matter. But as it is? Pfff...'

'So find something else.' Logan pulled the top four sheets out of the folder and laid them side-by-side on the desk. The first one was the latest missing person poster: a photo of Chris Browning sat beneath the headline, 'MISSING PERSON ~ APPEAL FOR INFORMATION'. He wasn't exactly a Hollywood heartthrob – a middle-aged man with pasty skin and a receding hairline, little round glasses and sunken eyes.

Steel clapped her hands together, then rubbed them. 'Of course, being *referendum day*, there's bound to be frayed tempers and a bit of a barney, right? Might get ourselves a one-punch-murder or two.'

A knock, and Rennie was back. 'Sorry, Guv. BBC coverage starts at ten: we're sending Guthrie out for pizza. You two want anything?'

She pointed at him. 'Did you vote like I told you?'

'Guv.'

'Good boy.' The finger came round to point at Logan. 'What about you?'

'None of your business.' The next sheet was a list of the most credible sightings from the last week. Which wasn't saying much. 'Now if you don't mind, I've got a missing person to find.'

'Pfff. No' really a person, is he? A lawyer, a pervert, a wannabe politician, *and* a No campaigner? The more of them goes missing the better.'

'Yes, because dehumanizing people who don't agree with you always turns out well.'

'Don't care. Sick of his smug, dumpy wee face. Banging away on the telly and the radio and the sodding papers,' she put on a posh Aberdonian accent, '"Scotland's going to fall apart under independence.", "We're not clever enough to run our own affairs without Westminster.", "You're all chip-eating, whisky-swigging, heart-attack-having, ginger-haired, tartan-faced, teuchter thickies, and you should be glad the posh boys in London are prepared to look after you."' She sniffed. 'Tosser.'

'You made that last one up.' Sheet number three held a photocopied article from the *Aberdeen Examiner*. 'MISSING CAMPAIGNER "PAID FOR SEX", CLAIM'. The journalist had got statements from a pair of working girls down on Regent Quay. Logan pulled out a pen, wrote the word 'NAMES?' and underlined it twice.

'And who cares what Chris Sodding Browning thinks anyway? Only reason the slimy git's getting airtime is because he was on that reality TV bollocks. *Silver City* my sharny arse. You want to make decent telly? Follow police officers about, no' some ambulance-chasing unionist turdbadger.'

'You finished?' The last sheet was a photocopy of Browning's diary for the day he went missing. Every appointment checked, everyone he'd met with interviewed. And still no idea where he was or what had happened to him. 'Chris Browning's perfectly entitled to support whatever side he wants. That's democracy.'

'Oh – my – God.' Steel took her feet off the windowsill and turned to face him. 'You're one of them, aren't you?'

'Eh?' Rennie frowned at Logan. 'Thought you liked girls, Guv? Not that there's anything wrong with it, but— Ow!'

Steel hit him again. 'No' one of *them*, you idiot, one of them: a Better Togetherer.' She shuddered. 'And to think I let you get my wife up the stick!'

Logan closed his eyes and folded forward, wrapped his hands around his face. 'Will you both, *please* bugger off?'

Rennie didn't. Instead he sat down in the other visitor's chair. 'Was great though, wasn't it? You know, that feeling of coming out of the polling station and thinking, "This is it. We could actually *do* this." Right? Wasn't it great?'

There was silence.

'Guv?'

Logan peeled one eye open.

Steel was sitting bolt upright in her seat, mouth hanging open. Then both eyebrows raised like drawbridges. 'What time is it?'

Rennie checked. 'Quarter to ten.'

She scrabbled to her feet. 'Get a car, *now*!'

2

The pool car roared its way up Schoolhill – past the closed shops – lights flashing, siren wailing. It still managed to sound better than Steel's rendition of 'Flower of Scotland', though.

She sat in the passenger seat, hanging onto the grab handle above the door as Rennie floored it.

Logan had to make do with his seatbelt, clutching it in both hands as the car flashed across the junction outside the Cowdray Hall, its granite lion watching with a silent snarl and a traffic cone on its head. The streetlight gilded it with a pale-yellow glow. He raised his voice over the wailing skirl. 'HOW COULD YOU FORGET TO VOTE?'

'IT'S NO' MY FAULT!'

'REALLY?'

'SHUT UP.'

Logan's mobile buzzed in his pocket, the ringtone drowned out by the siren. He pulled the phone out and hit the button. 'McRae.'

'*Guv?*' Stoney sounded as if he was standing at the bottom of a well. '*Hello? Guv? You there?*'

He leaned forward and poked Rennie in the shoulder. 'TURN THAT BLOODY THING OFF!'

But when Rennie reached for the controls, Steel slapped his hand away. 'DON'T YOU DARE!'

His Majesty's Theatre streaked by on the right – a chunk of green glass, followed by fancy granite, light blazing from its windows – then a church that looked like a bank, then the library. Granite. Granite. Granite.

'Guv? Hello?'

'I'LL CALL YOU BACK.' He hung up as the pool car jinked around the corner onto Skene Street, leaving a squeal of brakes behind. The headlights caught two pensioners, frozen on the central reservation, clutching each other as the car flashed by, dentures bared, eyes wide.

When Logan looked back, they'd recovered enough to make obscene gestures. 'STILL DON'T SEE WHY I NEED TO BE HERE.'

Steel waved a hand. 'IN CASE I NEED SOMEONE ARRESTED.'

Naked granite gave way to a shield of trees, their leaves dark and glistening in the streetlights.

Rennie pouted. 'I CAN ARREST PEOPLE!'

'COURSE YOU CAN. YOU'RE *VERY* SPECIAL. YES YOU ARE.' She turned in her seat and mugged at Logan. 'ISN'T IT SWEET WHEN THEY THINK THEY'RE REAL POLICE OFFICERS?'

'HOY!'

The pool car swept out and round a Transit van, then back in again. Slowed briefly for the junction outside the Grammar School, catching the lights at red, and back to full-speed-ahead, tearing up Carden Place. Granite. Granite. Granite.

She poked a finger at the windscreen. 'THERE!'

St Mary's Episcopal Church loomed on the left of the road. A vast, grand structure with lanced windows and buttresses. No tower. It occupied the triangular wedge between two roads, with expensive-looking cars parked along its kerbs.

15

Rennie slammed on the brakes and wrenched the steering wheel left. The back end kicked out for a moment, then they were lunging through the narrow gap between two spiky granite posts and scrunching to a halt on the gravel beyond. He flashed his watch. 'You've got one minute.'

Steel scrambled out of the car, sprinting across the gravel and in through the door marked 'POLLING STATION'.

'Cheeky old bag. I *am* a real police officer.'

'Sure you are.' Logan climbed into the warm night. Pulled out his phone and called Stoney back.

A couple of Yes campaigners stood off to one side, a couple of No on the other. Both sets waving Scottish flags and smiling at him. As if a flash of dodgy teeth and a bit of paper with lies on it was going to make a difference. Both sets marched toward him.

The Yes lot got there first – a young man with spots and a goatee. 'Good evening. Can I ask how you're planning to vote?'

'I'm on the phone.'

'Yes, but it'll only take a minute, won't it?'

His companion stuck her hands in the pockets of her tweed trousers. 'Going to have to get a shift on.' She pointed at the door. 'Polls close at ten.'

'*Guv?*'

Mr and Mrs No had appeared. One in a tracksuit, the other in a three-piece suit. Three-Piece turned his smile up an inch. 'Can we help?'

'I'm – on – the *phone*.' Logan turned his back and walked off a couple of paces. 'Stoney.'

Tracksuit sniffed. 'No need to be rude. We're only trying to help.'

'*Yeah, I've been on to the dayshift. Got a couple of sightings, but don't think they're up to much. One's in Torquay, one's in Nairn, and the other's in Lanzarote.*'

Three-Piece folded his arms. 'That's the trouble with Yes people. No manners.'

'Well, Chris Browning didn't go to Lanzarote. Not without his passport.'

Mr Spots folded his arms too, saltire flags sticking up like offensive weapons. 'Wait a minute – what makes you think he's one of ours?'

'Yeah.' Mrs Tweed poked Tracksuit in the chest. 'He was rude to us first.'

'Don't you poke me!'

'How come I can hear fighting?'

'I'm surrounded by idiots.' Logan held his phone against his chest. 'Sod off, the lot of you. I already voted, OK? Go bother someone else.' Back to Stoney. 'Get onto the *Aberdeen Examiner* and find out who fed them the story – I want to speak to their sources. We'll trawl the docks and see if anyone else saw Chris Browning down there.'

'You going to be back for the briefing?'

Mr Spots pursed his lips. 'Can I ask who you voted for?'

'No, you can't: sod off.'

'Guv?'

'Not you, Stoney, this lot.'

'So you voted No, then?'

'It's none of your business!' Logan jabbed a finger in the direction of Three-Piece and Tracksuit. 'And it's none of *their* business either. Now, for the last time: SOD OFF!' Bellowing out the last two words.

The four of them backed off, chins in, eyebrows up.

Three-Piece: 'Well, there was no need for that, was there?'

Mrs Tweed: 'No there wasn't.'

Tracksuit: 'There's always someone who lowers the debate to name calling, isn't there?'

Mr Spots: 'Honestly, some people think shouting's the same as democracy.'

17

Logan screwed his eyes shut. 'Stoney, if I'm up for four counts of murder tomorrow morning, can you feed my cat for me?'

'Deep breaths, Guv, count to ten.'

A smoky voice cut through the night. 'Ta-daaaaa!' And when Logan opened his eyes, there was Steel, bouncing on the top step with her arms up, like something out of a *Rocky* film. 'They canna take our FREEDOM!'

The little knot of idiots transferred their attentions her way.

'You want me to slide the briefing back a bit?'

Logan checked his watch again. 'Fifteen minutes. Then we hit the streets.'

3

The bells of some far off church tolled out a dozen chimes. Midnight.

Water Lane was narrow and dark, half the streetlights blown and broken. The cobbles slick beneath Logan's feet. Not that it'd been raining. No, they were all slippery with... Yeah, probably best *not* to think about what he'd just trodden in. Or on.

A tall granite building made a wall on one side of the lane, its guttering sprouting weeds, lichen on the lintels, broken windows. Boarded-up doors that opened onto nothing but fresh air on the second, third, and fourth floors. A couple of trees had burst out through the windows high up there, like slow-motion explosions.

The other side was more granite. Cold and unwelcoming. Not exactly the most romantic of spots for an intimate liaison. But then romance probably wasn't on the cards. Not even Richard Gere's character from *Pretty Woman* would have wheeched any of the working girls here off to a swanky hotel for pampering and shopping fun.

Two of them shuffled their feet, then looked away from the missing person poster in Logan's hand. One looked as if

19

she'd never see sixty again, but was probably barely out of her thirties. Her friend hadn't been at the drugs as long, so she still had all her own teeth and nowhere near as many pin-prick bruises up the inside of her arms. But they were both pipe-cleaner thin.

Logan sighed and tried again. 'Are you *sure* you've never seen him?'

The older one shook her head. 'Now, any chance you can sod off, only we've got quotas and that.'

Sugarhouse Lane was even narrower. The Regent Quay end was quiet – probably due to the half-dozen security cameras protecting the office buildings at the mouth of the alley. Further in, it was a different story. Blank granite topped with barbed wire on one side, warehouse-style walls on the other.

A lack of streetlights left the doorways and recesses in shadow.

Logan hunched his shoulders and stepped into the gloom.

The young man couldn't have been much over eighteen. If that. His red PVC T-shirt was dusty across the shoulders, his jeans torn and grubby about the knees. Every bit as thin and wobbly as the ladies of one street over. He licked his lips and stepped towards Logan. 'You looking for a good time, yeah?'

Logan pulled out the poster again. 'Looking for this man. You seen him?'

He lowered his head. 'Never seen no one...'

After a while, all the alleys blended into one another. Granite walls. Shadows. The smell of furtive sex and shame and desperation and barely-concealed violence.

Logan held the poster up and the woman with the thinning blonde hair shook her head. Same as the last five people he'd talked to.

As she clip-clopped away down the cobbles, Logan pulled out his phone and dialled Stoney. 'Anything?'

'Nah. It's like a Dress-Slutty Party for amnesiacs round here tonight. No one's seen him.'

'Well we know *two* people saw him. Has to be others.'

'Early days though, Guv. Maybe Elaine Mitchel and Jane Taylor don't come out till the clubs shut?'

Logan curled his lip and wandered back onto Regent Quay, with its warehouses, fences, and massive supply vessels, caught in the glare of security lighting. 'Don't fancy hanging about here till the back of three. Get onto Control – I want home addresses.'

'Guv.'

Till then, might as well complete the circuit and try Water Lane again.

Two steps in and Logan's phone launched into 'The Imperial March' from *Star Wars*. That would be Steel.

He pulled the phone out. 'What?'

'Too close to call, you believe that?'

'What is?'

'The referendum, you moron. They're showing all the ballot boxes arriving at the counting stations. Exit polls are too close to call.'

'Glad to hear you're working hard.'

'Don't be a dick. This is important.'

'Well, while you're sitting on your bum, watching TV, and eating pizza, I'm out searching the docks for witnesses. So if it's nothing urgent and police-related, feel free to be a pain in someone else's backside for a change.' He hung up and wandered further into the alley.

'This it?' Logan stood in the street and looked up. The tower block loomed in the darkness – twelve storeys of concrete and graffiti, a few lights shining from the upper floors. Wind whipped a broken newspaper against the chainlink fence, punishing it for its headline, 'A Dirty Campaign Of Fear And Lies?'

Stoney checked his notebook. 'Want to guess what floor?'

A groan. 'Top.'

'Yup.'

There was an intercom next to the double doors, half the metal cover missing, wires poking out. Didn't matter anyway – the door creaked open when Stoney nudged it with his foot. Then he flinched, nose crumped up on one side. 'Lovely. Eau De Toilette. Incontinence, *pour homme*.'

Deep breaths.

They marched inside. A faded cardboard sign was duct taped to the lift's dented doors. 'Out Of Order'.

Damn right it was.

They took the stairs. Dark stains clustered at every landing, the nipping reek of ammonia strong enough to make Logan's eyes water. Go faster and be out of it quicker, but then there would be puffing and panting and breathing more of it in...

When finally they arrived on the twelfth floor, Stoney was a coughing, wheezing lump. Dragging air in. And Logan wasn't much better. By rights, the top floors should've been less stinky, shouldn't they? People would pee on their way downstairs, or on their way back to their flats. No one headed *upstairs* to pee, did they?

Stoney wafted a hand in front of his face. 'God's sake, stairwell must run like Niagara Falls on a Saturday night.' He coughed a couple of times, then spat. Wiped his mouth. 'That's it at the end.'

Flat four still had its number attached to the red-painted door. The word 'HOORS!' was sprayed across the wood in three-foot tall letters. If it was advertising, it wasn't working. After slogging all the way up here, who'd have the energy to do anything?

Logan knocked.

Waited.

Knocked again.

Had a third go.

Finally, a voice on the other side, thin and muffled. *'Go away, or I'll call the police! I know who your mothers are!'*

OK...

'I can save you the trouble – it *is* the police.'

Silence.

Stoney puffed out his cheeks. 'Can we not sod about here, madam? It's a long way to climb and it stinks of pish.'

The door cracked open an inch and a slice of pale skin appeared in the gap. The eye was grey, the iris circled in white. Chamois-leather creases across the cheek. 'How do I know you're policemen?'

Logan showed her his warrant card, then Stoney did the same. She peered myopically at them, then grunted and closed the door again. Unlatched the chain. A pink cardigan slumped over a thin, hunched frame. Pink scalp showing through thin yellowy hair. She turned and led the pair of them through a stripped-bare hallway into the living room.

No carpet. No underlay. A tatty brown couch against one wall, a pile of dirty washing against the other. And in-between, a panoramic window that looked out across Aberdeen. A sky of ink, the streetlights glowing firefly ribbons. It would have been breathtaking, if the climb and sudden smell of cat hadn't already taken care of that.

An overflowing litter tray bulged in the corner, like a heaped display of miniature black puddings.

A large ginger cat sat in the middle of the couch, bright orange with a shining white bib and paws, as if he'd been painted with marmalade and Tipp-Ex. How the cat managed to stay so clean in this manky hole was anyone's guess. It raised its nose and sniffed at the scruffy pair of police officers, somehow implying that Logan and Stoney were the ones responsible for the horrible smell.

The woman sat down next to her cat and stroked its back, getting a deep rumbling purr in return. 'Whatever they told you, I didn't do it.' She kissed the cat's head. 'Did I, Mr Seville? No, Mummy didn't do nothing.'

Stoney took out his notebook. 'Didn't do what?'

She sniffed and looked out of the window. 'They shout horrible things at me when I get my messages. I'm not well. They could kill me. One of the wee shites tried to kick Mr Seville! What kind of person does that? Should be locked up.'

Logan went to lean back against the wall, then caught himself and stood up straight again before anything could stain. 'Elaine Mitchel and Jane Taylor. They live here?'

Hard to believe that *anyone* lived here.

'I'm an old woman. I deserve better than this.'

A rat deserved better than this.

'Are they in?'

A shrug. 'They come and go, I'm not their mother.' She pulled up the sleeve of her cardigan for a scratch, and there they were: the tell-tale bruises and scabs of a long-term intravenous drug user. 'Were supposed to get me some cider and ciggies.' She scratched. Licked her lips. Scratched again. 'You got any ciggies?'

Stoney dipped into his pocket for a packet of menthol, then cracked open a window, letting in the gentle hum of the city. Lit one of the cigarettes and handed it over.

She took it and pulled, cheeks hollow, the end glowing and sizzling. Holding the smoke in for a beat, before letting it out in a post-orgasmic sigh. 'They're good girls. They look after their Aunty Ina.'

Stoney put his cigarettes away. 'How long they been on the gamc?'

'Go' to make ends meet, haven't we? God knows we get sod all off the welfare state.'

Logan opened his mouth, then closed it again. Her use of the plural there wasn't exactly conjuring up a happy image. 'We need to speak to them. They're not in trouble, we just need to ask them some questions about something they saw.'

The eyes brightened. 'There a reward?'

'No.'

'Oh.' She sat back again and stroked her pristine cat. 'Are you sure?'

'The Imperial March' blared out from Logan's pocket. 'Sorry,' he pointed over his shoulder at what looked like the kitchen door, 'can I take this in there?'

'Free country. Long as your pal gives us another ciggie.'

Logan slipped through into a galley kitchen that looked as if it'd been decorated by someone on a dirty protest. Though, presumably, it was food smeared up the walls. Please let it be food. A bin was heaped with ready-meal cartons and boxes, spilling out onto the floor and worktop. Cheap supermarket value own-brand lasagne, burgers, sausages, shepherd's pie... Mystery meat and gristle with added sugar and salt.

The sink was heaped with dishes and cutlery. A thick dusting of dead bluebottles on the windowsill filled the space between empty supermarket-whisky bottles. A single clean patch was reserved for a placemat on the floor with three bowls on it. One water, the others heaped with glistening brown food. Going by the empty pouches on the cooker, Mr Seville was eating better than the people. The cat's meals certainly cost a lot more.

Logan stood as far away from the units and surfaces as possible and pulled out his phone. 'What?'

'*Sodding Clackmannanshire, that's what! Fifty-four percent "No", forty-six percent "Yes". What's wrong with people?*'

He closed his eyes and massaged the bridge of his nose. 'Did you call me up to tell me that?'

'First result and it's a "No". Half one and we've already got a sodding deficit of nearly three thousand votes to make up!'

'Go away.'

'Laz, have you got any idea—'

He hung up, but the phone blared its Imperial theme at him again. He hit the button. 'I'm *working.*'

'Dundee turnout's only seventy-nine percent. If every bugger had bothered their arse and showed up, that'd be another twenty-five thousand votes, right there! It—'

He hung up again. Scrolled through the menu system before she could call back and blocked her number.

At least now he might get some sodding peace.

Back in the living room, Aunty Ina was well down her second cigarette, while Stoney leaned back against the windowsill. The cat paused, then went back to washing an immaculate pink-padded paw.

Stoney nodded at the kitchen. 'Something important, Guv?'

'No.' He stood in front of the couch. 'We any nearer?'

'Ina here says we can search Elaine and Jane's room for twenty quid.'

She smiled. 'Seeing as they're family, and that.'

4

Stoney had a wee shudder as he straightened up and made rubber spiders with his blue-nitriled fingers. 'I'm not even going to *try* to describe what it's like under the bed.'

Aunty Ina stood in the doorway, another one of Stoney's cigarettes poking out of the side of her mouth, the big ginger cat clasped to her chest like a purring baby. 'Aye, they're a bit manky right enough.'

A *bit* manky?

The room was an open landfill site for dirty clothes, takeaway containers, and abandoned gossip magazines. They made drifts in the corners, were piled up around the double bed, avalanched out of the battered wardrobe. It smelled like the inside of an old sock in here, one that had been marinated in cannabis resin and sweat.

Logan tried his luck with the chest of drawers in the corner. The top one creaked out with a groan. Nothing but cheap-looking frilly pants. Some of which hadn't been washed.

'Course, they take after their mum. Never met a bigger slag in your life than Morag.'

Next drawer: socks tied in tight little bundles.

'So Morag's up the stick with Elaine, and she and

27

Whatsisname get married. Registry office. Couldn't wear white, could she? Not when half the school'd had a go.' Aunty Ina took a drag and blew a lungful of smoke at the stained ceiling. 'Didn't last. Well, hard to be a dad when you've got a paper round, isn't it?'

Next drawer: baby toys. Rattles, dummies, shaky things in the shape of flowers, a stars-and-moon mobile still in the packaging. A pink fuzzy cat. A tiny romper suit with orange and black stripes like a tiger. He pulled the tiger costume out and held it up. 'Does Elaine or Jane have a child?' Because if they did, Social Services were getting a call to rescue it from this rancid hovel.

Aunty Ina stuck the cigarette back in her mouth and shifted her grip on her cat. 'Naw, that's Elaine's. Silly cow thinks she'll be a *wonderful* mummy someday. As if. Collects this crap the whole time. Got bags of it in the wardrobe.'

Yeah, because *that* wasn't creepy.

'Anyway,' Ina rubbed Mr Seville's tummy, 'then along comes Shuggie and sweeps Morag off her feet. Come with me, baby, we'll see the world...' A sigh. 'Real looker he was too.'

Last drawer. It was full of carrier bags.

'Course, she's full of herself. "Oh, he loves me. Oh, he'll do anything for me. Oh, we're so happy." And six weeks later, she's got a broken arm, a broken nose, she's pregnant – *again* – and Shuggie's shacked up with some other poor cow.'

Logan tipped the first one out on the bare mattress. An assortment of watches spilled out onto the stained fabric. A few still had the price stickers attached.

'Eight years later, and she's overdosed in a squat and I'm lumbered with her bloody kids. Some sister, eh?'

The next bag contained cheap jewellery, the kind sold at the tills in Markies and BHS. All plastic and shiny bits. All still pinned to rectangles of cardboard.

'Lucky the wee buggers didn't end up in care.'

28

Logan looked around the horrible little room Elaine and Jane shared in the horrible little flat, with their horrible little aunt. 'Yeah, *really* lucky.'

Bag number three was full of cosmetics from Boots – own-brand stuff, probably snatched off the shelves while no one was looking.

Aunty Ina finished her cigarette and pinged the butt away into the piles of dirty clothes. Then rubbed her ginger baby between the ears. 'If you find any money, it's mine. They borrowed it.'

Bag number four was different. It contained a parcel of white powder – about the size of a mealie pudding – wrapped up in layers of clingfilm and secured with strips of parcel tape. 'Well, well, well.'

Little beads of dark red had dried on the plastic surface, like ladybirds.

'The lying wee shites!' Aunty Ina stamped a foot on the bare floorboards, making Mr Seville wriggle in her arms. 'They told me they didn't have any gear!'

The patrol car pulled up outside the tower block, lights spinning in the darkness, and sat there.

Logan stepped out from the block's shadow and rapped on the driver's window. 'You sitting there for a reason?'

Constable Haynes smiled up at him, then fluttered her eyelashes. 'Wanted to make sure it was safe, Guv. I leave Wee Billy here unsupervised for five minutes, might come back to find someone's nicked his boots and truncheon. He's only new.'

Her partner, sitting in the passenger seat, blushed – gritting his teeth and saying nothing, like a big boy.

Logan pointed up at Aunty Ina's flat. 'Top floor. No lift. Make sure the auld wifie stays put till we get the Procurator Fiscal organised. Soon as you're *there*, tell DC Stone he's wanted back *here*. And while you're at it—' His phone launched into its anonymous ringtone. 'Hold on.' He pulled it out and pressed the button. 'McRae.'

'Seven morons in Clackmananshire voted "Yes" and "No" on the same ballot paper. You believe that? How thick can they be?'

He closed his eyes. 'It's you.'

'Couldn't get through on my phone. Had to borrow one. Sodding Glasgow's seventy-five percent turnout. Seventy-five percent! What sodding use is that? Even Aberdeen managed eighty-two.'

'Stop calling me with numbers, OK? I – don't – care. I'm *working.*'

'Seventy-five percent. How many thousands of votes is that lost? Eh? You know what I think? I think—'

Logan hung up. Barred that number too.

Haynes pulled her bowler down low on her head, leaving the fringes of her bob showing. 'Let me guess, Detective Chief Inspector Steel?'

Her partner clambered out of the car, all sticky-out ears and chin. 'She's driving everyone mental back at the ranch. Stand still for two minutes and she'll get you working out percentages and stuff. Nightmare. Like being back at school.'

Logan punched the duty superintendent's number into his mobile and wandered over to the pool car he and Stoney had arrived in, settling back against the bonnet while it rang.

Then a large, sharp voice battered out of the earpiece. *'Superintendent Ward.'*

'Sir? DI McRae. Just found a block of what looks like coke in a flat.'

'You have a search warrant?'

'Permission from the householder. We were looking for the two women who said they'd seen Chris Browning on the fourth. Their aunt told us we could search the place if we liked.'

'Hmmm… Let me have a word with the PF. Everyone still in situ?'

'Left DC Stone with the aunt, sir. Uniform's just arrived.'

30

'Good. Right. I'll let you know.'

And with any luck, that would be enough to cover Logan and Stoney's backsides when it got to court. Logan slipped his phone into his pocket, and settled back to wait.

Langstane Place bustled with staggery groups of men and women, calling and whooping to each other. A handful of Temporary Public Urination Stations, AKA: Daleks, had been set up along the road. Big dark plastic things, with four semi-private bays for people to pee in. Not exactly classy, but it was better than them doing it in shop doorways.

Stoney checked his watch. 'Twenty to.'

Logan sucked on his teeth for a bit. 'Don't see them, do you?'

'I remember when this was nothing but houses and churches. Now look at it.'

'Showing your age, Stoney. Got to move with the times.'

The place was one long ribbon of nightclubs, all heaving with referendum night parties. Blootered voters, trying their luck with members of the opposite sex. Offering to stuff each other's ballot boxes.

Aunty Ina had named a couple of places where her nieces usually plied their trade on a Thursday night. Regent Quay was one of them, this was the other.

Logan pulled out another printout of Elaine and Jane, both from the police database, looking straight forward with a height chart behind them. He held it up for the bouncer outside Sneaky Jimmy's – a slab of muscle with a number-one buzz cut and tattoos up her neck. 'You seen either of these women?'

She narrowed her eyes and peered at the sheet. Then turned and waved her companion over. He wasn't as big as she was, but his scalp looked as if a Rottweiler had been chewing on it, scar tissue showing through the severe haircut.

31

'Marky, you seen this pair tonight?'

He bared his teeth and sooked a breath through them. 'Aye.' A finger like a sausage poked the paper. 'This one was minesweeping. Nicking other people's drinks when they wasn't looking. This one,' he poked the other photo, 'got into a fight in the ladies. Had to throw the pair of them out on their arses.' He raised an arm, then pulled up his shiny black bomber jacket, exposing a circle of red across his ribs. 'Cow bit me, and everything.'

Stoney tutted. 'Better get that looked at, mate. Don't want to catch anything.'

Logan took the printout back. 'When was this?'

'About twenty minutes ago? Something like that?'

And they hadn't been into any of the other nightclubs, so that really only left one place. Back to the docks.

'Thanks.' He turned and his phone launched into 'If I Only Had a Brain'. That would be Rennie. He followed Stoney back to the pool car and hit the button. 'McRae.'

A smoky growl sounded in his ear. *'Are you avoiding me?'*

Oh God, not her *again*.

'Yes. Take the hint.'

'Orkney: sixty-seven percent "No", thirty-three "Yes". Bloody Shetland's no better: sixty-four, thirty-six. What are we—'

'Have you done any work at all tonight?'

There was a pause. *'Might have done.'*

'Yeah, well I've recovered about a quarter kilo of cocaine. Go do something productive for a change.'

'No point. Shift ends in fifteen. Fancy hitting the pub?'

For goodness sake. He drummed his fingers on the car roof as Stoney unlocked it. 'I'm on *nights*, remember? Don't get off till seven.'

'Aye, well, there'll still be places open. I'm going to hang about and inspire the troops.'

Oh joy.

5

'What do you think, Guv – call it a night?' Stoney stuck his hands in his pockets and drew a foot along the double yellow line on Shore Lane.

Logan pulled his sleeve back and angled his watch so the streetlight's sickly glow caught the dial. 'Better give it till four. Make sure everyone's had time to stagger down here from the nightclubs.'

Besides, with any luck, Steel would have given up by then and sodded off home, leaving everyone in peace.

Shore Lane stretched from Regent Quay to the dual carriageway on the other side, where the occasional lonely taxi drifted by on its way somewhere much nicer than this. A canyon of granite, punctuated by darkened windows and downpipes.

Stoney puffed out a breath – just visible in the night air – then shrugged. 'Might as well get on with it, I suppose.' He turned and wandered down the lane, making for the dual carriageway.

Logan headed back to Regent Quay instead. A couple of flats had their lights on, probably sitting up watching the results come in, but mostly it was darkness. On the other side of the harbour wall, the security lights blazed, making the vast orange vessels glow.

The Regents Arms was still open though, one of those harbour pubs with an all-night licence for the shift workers. The sort of place you could get a sausage buttie and a pint of Guinness at six in the morning. The sort of place you could get your head kicked in for looking at someone funny. Even if you *were* a police officer.

A figure stood outside the door, hunched over, one hand cupped around a cigarette as if someone was going to snatch it off him if he lowered his guard. Cardigan, jeans, slippers, a nose that could prize open tin cans. He nodded as Logan passed, setting a mop of grey hair swinging. 'Inspector.'

'Donald.'

And past.

The *clang, clang, clang* of something metal getting battered with a hammer came from the harbour. A people carrier drove past. Somewhere in the distance, someone launched into a mournful and tuneless rendition of 'My Love is like a Red, Red Rose'.

Logan turned the corner onto Water Lane, for about the ninth time that night.

Halfway down, beneath a broken streetlamp, a couple of figures huddled in the gloom. One tall, one not so much. Little more than silhouettes, caught in the glow of the dual carriageway behind. Then the shorter one sank down to its knees while the taller one leaned back against the wall.

No prizes for guessing what was going on there, then.

Hopefully whoever was on their knees had been paid in advance, because unless the tall guy was a *really* quick finisher, there wasn't going to be time to negotiate afterwards.

Logan marched down the cobblestones. Reached into his pocket for his LED torch.

Got within thirty feet, then clicked it on.

A harsh cone of bright white stabbed through the darkness, catching a bald man with his trousers and pants around his knees, head thrown back; and a skeletal woman on her knees, head bobbing at his crotch.

Logan took a deep breath. 'POLICE!'

Mr Tall jerked upright. Spluttering, mouth stretched out like a dying frog. 'Shite!' He shoved the woman away, and he was off, lurching and scrambling as fast as he could with his trousers hobbling him.

The woman hit the cobblestones with a crack.

And twenty seconds later, so did Mr Tall – betrayed by his treacherous trousers. He careened into the road with arms and legs flailing. Scrambled to his knees, pulled himself upright, hauled his trousers into a more acceptable position, and ran for it.

Logan let him go. Stood over the fallen woman and offered her a hand up.

She scowled at him. Her cheekbones were razor sharp, her eyes hollow and dark, quick-bitten fingernails and a tremor that made everything shake. 'You think that was *funny*?'

'You get the cash upfront?'

'Could've killed me.'

'Look on the bright side: you got paid and you don't have to do the deed.'

Elaine Mitchel sniffed. Then wiped her nose on the sleeve of her jacket, adding to the silver trails. She turned her head, staring off down the darkened lane after her departed customer. A strangler's ring of love bites encircled her throat. 'True.'

Logan helped her up. 'Been looking for you all night.' Then pulled out the missing person poster. 'You recognise this man?'

Her eyes flicked towards the poster, then away again. 'Don't remember, like.' Heat radiated from her bony chest, taking with it a smell of stale perfume and sweat.

Logan shone his torch on the poster, so the picture was nice and clear. 'Come on, have another look'.

She did, but only for the briefest of beats. 'Don't remember.'

'Chris Browning, forty-two, brown hair, glasses, slightly posh Aberdonian accent.'

She took a step away. 'Got stuff to do.'

Logan grabbed her arm. It was barely there – just a length of bone, wrapped in snot-streaked material, burning into his palm. 'His family's worried, OK?'

Elaine looked down at Logan's hand, then up to his face. 'You want to touch me, you gotta pay.'

He let go. 'Come on, Elaine, no one's seen him for two weeks. You told Jimmy from the *Aberdeen Examiner* that you saw Chris Browning on the fourth. You said he was a regular.'

She stared at her shoes – high heels, the leather all scuffed and stained. 'Don't remember. Didn't talk to no journo.'

'Jimmy *named* you, Elaine. Gave up his source, just like that.'

Her thin lips disappeared inside her mouth, creases forming between her eyebrows. 'Don't remember.'

A pair of headlights paused at the entrance to the lane … and then drifted past. Not this time.

'OK. I understand.' Logan nodded. 'Elaine Mitchel, I'm detaining you under Section Fourteen of the—'

'No.' She backed up, until she was against the wall. 'I don't…' She threw her arms out to the sides. 'Could you not leave us alone?'

'Section Fourteen of the Criminal Procedure – Scotland – Act 1995, because I suspect you of having committed an offence punishable by imprisonment. You—'

'OK! OK.' A sigh. 'OK. I never met the man.' She pointed at the poster. 'Him.'

'You told Jimmy that Chris Browning was down here every Wednesday, paying for, and I quote, "Disgusting and unusual sex acts".'

One bony shoulder came up to her ear, then fell again. 'Never met him.'

'Then why say you did?'

'Money.' She smiled at Logan, all twisted brown teeth and beige gums. 'A *hundred* quid.'

The wall behind the bar was festooned with stolen apostrophes. Some were large and plastic, some small and metal, some neon, others designed to be illuminated by whoever paid for them in the first place, not knowing that some wee sod from Aberdeen was going to wheech up a ladder with a screwdriver in the middle of the night and make off with their punctuation.

The barman took one look at Logan and sighed. Then raised his voice, so the dozen people spread in ones and twos about the place could hear over the telly playing in the corner of the room. 'Detective Inspector, what can I get you?'

Subtle.

Logan pointed at Elaine Mitchel. 'You?'

'Double vodka.'

'And a tin of Irn-Bru.'

The barman clunked a glass up beneath the optic, twice, then dumped it on the bar. 'You want a glass with the Irn-Bru?'

And give him something to spit in? 'No thanks. Tin's fine.'

It was produced, and Logan paid the man, then led the way across to a table in the corner, away from the speakers. Sitting with his back to the wall, just in case.

He wiped a thumb across the tin's top, clearing off the sheen of dew, then clicked the ringpull off. 'A hundred quid's a lot of money.'

Elaine shrugged, then took a sip. Holding the vodka in her mouth with her eyes closed. Savouring it.

'Who paid?'

She swallowed. Sighed. 'A man. Same as usual.'

'You know who he is?'

Elaine shifted in her seat, looking back at the television with its array of BBC journalists and pundits sitting behind a big curved desk. 'Any idea how it's going?'

'Do you know who paid you? Did you get a name?'

'We did a postal vote. Just in case, you know? Wanted to make sure it counted.' Another sip of vodka.

Up on the screen, they were scrolling through the results so far. 'WESTERN ISLES: "No". 53% To 47%. INVERCLYDE: "No". 50.1% To 49.9%.'

Steel would *love* that.

'Elaine. I need a name, or I can't help you.'

She picked at the table, where someone had carved the initials DG into the wood. 'Who says I need help? Doing fine, aren't I?'

'We were at your aunt's place tonight. She showed us your room.'

Elaine turned back to the television. 'Going to be no, isn't it? Probably just as well.'

'Want to guess what we found in your chest of drawers? Right at the bottom, with all the shoplifted watches, makeup, and costume jewellery?'

'What'd happen to all the benefits, eh? Who's going to pay our dole: BP and Shell? My arse.'

'We found about a quarter kilo of cocaine, Elaine. About, what, a good ten, twelve grand's worth?'

'Then there's all the supermarkets putting up their prices, and the banks sodding off down south, and the other big companies...'

'That's possession with intent.'

'And they'll close the border. Be like, a big stretch of barbed wire from Grenta to Berwick-upon-Tweed. Guard towers and spotlights and Alsatians and ghettos...'

'You're looking at nine to thirteen years, Elaine.'

She sniffed. Polished off her vodka. 'Isn't mine. Found it.'

He sat back. 'Here we go.'

'Nope, it's the God's. Me and Jane found it, down the Green. Can't bang us up if it isn't ours.'

'You *found* a quarter kilo of cocaine lying about in the Green?'

'Na. Yeah.' The bony shoulders rose and fell. 'Kinda. This bloke was doing a runner, right? Battering it down Correction Wynd, under the bridge hell-for-leather into the Green. Got a nose like a burst bottle of ketchup, blood all down the front of his shirt. He dumps this padded envelope in a bin and keeps going. Thirty seconds later, these three big bastards hammer after him. Caught him outside Granite Reef and pounded the crap out of him.'

Logan's eyebrow climbed up his forehead. 'When was this?'

'Dunno. Tuesday?'

It was the assault Steel couldn't be bothered investigating because an Edinburgh drug dealer getting beaten up wasn't 'major' enough. And it explained what the little dark-red spots on the package of coke were. Blood.

'You see who did it?'

'Depends. It worth something?'

'Nine to thirteen years. You help me, I help you.'

She stuck a finger in her empty glass and wiped up the last smears of alcohol. Sooked it clean. 'You know Alec Hadden: drinks in here sometimes?'

'He one of them?'

Elaine shook her head. 'He's the one gave me and Jane a hundred quid to say that Chris Browning was a regular. Told us to say the guy was into all kinds of filthy stuff, you know? Real pervert scumbag. Likes it rough up the bum and that.'

Logan looked over her shoulder, taking in the assembled slouch of wee-small-hours drinkers. 'This Alec in tonight?'

She checked. 'Nah. Doesn't usually come in till five or six, though. Think he works up the hospital or something, doesn't get off till then.' Elaine smiled at him, exposing a lopsided jumble of brown teeth. 'If we're waiting, any chance of another voddie?'

Something buzzed in Logan's pocket. 'Hold on.' He pulled it out: text message.

> I love Dundee!!!
> Yes: 57%!!! Wee dancers!
> I'm never making fun of Dundee ever again.
> Dundee! Dundee! Dundee!

That would be Steel, hijacking someone else's phone again. Well, at least she was happy for a change. The phone vibrated in his fingers.

> Well, maybe not never ever, it is Dundee after all.

And again.

> Sodding Renfrewshire is No: 53%
> Tossers.

How could she type so fast with her thumbs?

He put his phone on the table and Elaine jerked her head towards the bar.

'So… Vodka?'

'Nope: station.'

That brown smile died. 'But—'

'A quarter kilo of cocaine, remember?' He stood. 'You need to make a statement, or you need to go to prison. Your choice. But either way there's no more vodka in it.'

She slumped right down, until her top half rested on the table. 'Noooo…'

'How about this: you help me catch the guys who beat up the drug dealer, and I'll buy you a whole bottle?'

There was a small pause, then she dragged herself to her feet. 'Better than nothing.'

6

There was a knock on the interview room door, then Stoney appeared. 'Guv?'

His moustache was slightly ... lopsided. A scrape on his cheek. What looked like the beginnings of an excellent shiner spreading beneath his right eye.

Logan frowned. 'Detective Constable Stone enters the room.'

Sitting on the other side of the table, Elaine slumped to one side. 'Can I go for a pee?'

'In a minute.' Logan pointed. 'What happened to you?'

'Gah...' His mouth stretched out and down. 'Jane Taylor happened. Had to drop her off at the hospital, couldn't even stand, she was so drunk. Didn't stop her though.' He fingered the bruise beneath his eye. 'Like a blootered Mike Tyson.'

'Yeah, Janey always did take after her dad.' Elaine's feet drummed on the grey floor. 'Seriously, I'm *bursting* here.'

What the hell. 'Interview suspended at four twenty-two. DC Stone, can you escort Miss Mitchel to the bathroom and back again. Ten minutes.'

He backed off a pace. 'She doesn't bite, does she?'

That brown smile was back. 'Not unless you pay extra.'

*   *   *

42

Logan took a sip from his polystyrene cup on the way back to his office. The coffee from the machine wasn't great at the best of times, but there was something about drinking it out of expanded hydrocarbon foam that really classed it up. Could always sneak into the MIT office and help himself to their stash. After all, they'd all have gone home for the night.

He dumped the cup in the nearest bin and made for the stairs. Taking them two at a time up to the next floor. Pushed through the door into the Major Investigation Team's domain.

Stopped.

So much for sneaking a go on their fancy coffee machine in secret.

Half a dozen plainclothes officers lounged in office chairs, all facing the large flatscreen TV at the front of the room, watching the BBC's live coverage. The interactive whiteboard was divided up into a grid – percentages and numbers across the top, the name of each Scottish region down the side.

The office was easily six times bigger than the grubby hovel the CID had been relegated to. Here they had new desks. New chairs. New ceiling tiles. A carpet that didn't look as if a herd of incontinent sheep had rampaged across it for twenty years. New computers. State-of-the-art tech kit. And right at the back, one of those fancy coffee machines that took wee pod cartridges and produced something that didn't taste of boiled slurry.

Steel had pride of place, surrounded by her minions, a bottle of Grant's Whisky open on the desk beside her, next to a pizza box containing a couple of congealed slices. She took a sip and scowled at him. 'West Dumbartonshire: fifty-four percent "Yes", forty-six "No".'

'That's good, isn't it?' Might as well brass neck it. He wandered over to the coffee machine and plucked a cartridge at random. Stuck it in the machine.

43

'No' good enough. Sodding Stirling was sixty percent "No". *Sixty.'*

The machine churned and groaned and chugged.

Steel pointed at a bloke in a stripy shirt and undone tie. 'Colin?'

He nodded, blinked in slow motion, then squinted at the whiteboard. 'Midlothian fifty-six percent "No". East Lothian: sixty-two percent "No". Falkirk: fifty-three percent "No".'

Steel waved a hand. 'Shut up, they're doing Angus. Come on Angus, do it for Aunty Roberta...'

Up on the screen, a man with almost no hair above his ears stood behind a podium, in front of an Angus Council display board. *'... the total number of rejected votes was sixty-six and the reasons for rejection were as follows. Seventeen for voting for both answers—'*

'How? How could anyone be that stupid? It's a yes or no sodding question!'

'The total number of votes cast in relation to each answer to the referendum question, in this area, was as follows...'

'Stop milking it and read the sodding result!'

'"Yes": thirty-five thousand and forty-four. "No": forty-five thousand one hundred and ninety-two. That concludes this evening's count.'

'Noooooooooooo!' Steel buried her head in her hands. 'Sodding hell.'

Logan grabbed his coffee and slipped out before she resurfaced.

Elaine yawned, showing off those crooked brown teeth again. Most of them boasted a shiny grey chunk of dentist's jewellery. Then she sagged in her seat. 'We about done?'

'Just a couple more things.' Logan turned the ID book around so it faced her. 'Can you identify the fourth man?'

She sighed, then jabbed a finger at the page, selecting a

hairy man with tiny squinty eyes and a nose that pointed at his left cheek. 'Him.'

'And you're certain?'

'Said so, didn't I?'

'Right.' Logan copied Captain Hairy's name into his notebook. 'For the record, Miss Mitchel has identified Dominic Walker as the fourth assailant. And that's it?'

She nodded. 'Can I sod off now?'

'One more.' Logan closed the book, then checked his notes. 'I need an ID for Alec Hadden – the guy who paid you to lie about Chris Browning being one of your regulars.'

Elaine shrugged one shoulder. 'Tell you what, Regents Arms is open till nine. How about we go back there and wait till he turns up?' She licked her lips with a pale, dead-slug tongue. 'Get a couple of drinks. Get a bit friendlier...?'

Sitting next to him, Stoney flinched. 'Gah!'

Logan frowned at him. 'You OK?'

Colour rushed up his cheeks. 'She's playing footsy under the table, Guv. Came as a bit of a shock.'

Took all sorts. 'Interview suspended at four forty-five so Constable Stone can assist Miss Mitchel with the production of an identikit picture of Alec Hadden.' Logan switched off the recorder and stood. 'No funny business.'

'Guv, it wasn't—'

'Now: none of that. You keep your galloping hormones to yourself.' He left them to it, pulling out his phone and dialling with his thumb as he made his way back to the office. 'Guthrie? It's Logan. My office: I want you to run some PNC checks.'

'Guv.'

By the time he got there, PC Guthrie was already waiting, like an expectant golden retriever. Logan scribbled down names for each of the four thugs Elaine Mitchel had IDed then added 'Alec Hadden' at the bottom. 'Full check on the lot of them. Then get onto the hospital and see when they think Jane Taylor's going to be sober enough to interview.'

'Guv.' He stood there, clutching the sheet of paper.

'Run along then.'

'Oh, right.'

Logan settled behind his desk and pulled over the phone. Put in a call to Aberdeen Royal Infirmary. But no one there had heard of Alec Hadden. Was he sure he'd got the name right? Not really. Ah well, better luck next time.

Worth a try though.

He logged back into his computer, getting the paperwork started for a warrant to arrest the guys who'd battered the drug dealer from Edinburgh. Assuming they could get Jane Taylor to corroborate her sister's IDs, that was. Be hard to convince a sheriff to give them a warrant on the say so of a single addict. Two: yes, one: no.

There was a knock on the door, and Stoney stuck his head in. The shiner was darkening nicely beneath his eye. 'Guv?' He held up a printout. 'Alec Hadden.'

Wow.

'That was fast.'

'Used my initiative, Guv, and googled him.' Stoney put the printout on the desk. It was a photo of a thin man with shoulder-length brown hair and a broad grin, underneath the headline, 'LOCAL MAN IS WORLD PORRIDGE CHAMPION'.

'*World* porridge champion. La-dee-dah.'

'Bet he keeps the trophy where everyone can see it too. Looks the type, doesn't he?'

'OK. He's supposed to be at the Regents Arms sometime after five. Probably better keep it low key – last thing we need's a brawl kicking off in there.'

Stoney grimaced. 'You sure we can't call in the Riot Brigade? Regents Arms isn't exactly cop-friendly.'

'Low key does *not* mean shields, battering rams, and crash

helmets. We'll go with you, me, and Wheezy Doug… What?'

'Wheezy's got court tomorrow. Went home at midnight, remember?'

'OK, when Guthrie's done with the PNC checks, tell him to change into civvies. We're going down the pub.'

7

'Dear God, it's Action Man!' Stoney rocked back on his heels as PC Guthrie appeared in the corridor.

He'd changed out of his police-ninja black into a pair of cargo pants, green jumper with patches on the elbows and shoulders, and finished the ensemble off with a pair of big black boots. 'What?'

'Go on, do the kung fu grip thing.'

Logan hit Stoney. 'Don't mock the afflicted. Everyone ready?'

All three of them produced their handcuffs, and wee CS gas canisters. Then Guthrie dug into one of his many trouser pockets and came out with a canister of Bite Back. 'Just in case.'

'Good boy.' Logan put his cuffs away. 'Right, let's do it. We can... What?'

Stoney was staring over his shoulder. 'Guv?'

Then a smoky voice of doom grated out behind. 'Gah! It's all *ruined*.'

Logan didn't bother turning around. What was the point? 'Detective Chief Inspector Steel, I presume.'

She sniffed. 'Sodding Aberdeen City. How *could* you?' The words were a little slurred at the edges. 'Cowardly bastards.'

Stoney winced. 'More "No"s?'

'The sodding BBC have called it. Twenty-six out of thirty-two local authorities so far, and only four voted "Yes". *Four.* Two hundred and thirty *thousand* votes down. No way we can come back from this. It's over and Scotland bottled it!' A hand slapped down on Logan's shoulder. 'Laz, I think we need to go get very, very drunk.'

Stoney grinned. 'Funny you should say that, we're off to— Ow! You kicked me!'

Logan kept his eyes on Steel. 'We're away to pick up a suspect.'

She narrowed her eyes. 'You're a lying wee sod.' She poked him in the chest and leaned in, enveloping him in second-hand whisky fumes. 'Where are you off to?'

Guthrie stuck up his hand. 'The Regents Arms. Going to arrest someone.'

Steel beamed and threw her arms wide. 'Perfect! I'll come supervise.'

'Oh no you don't.' Logan backed towards the exit. 'You're off duty, and you've been drinking. You're supervising nobody.'

'Fine.' She dropped her arms and narrowed her eyes. 'Be like that.' Then she turned and marched off down the corridor. 'But don't say I didn't warn you.'

Wonderful.

The same auld mannie was standing outside the Regents Arms, smoking another furtive cigarette in his slippers. He nodded as Logan stepped up to the door. 'Inspector.'

'Donald.'

Inside, the number of patrons out for a pre-dawn booze-up had swelled to twenty. All nursing drinks. Their sour faces turned to watch as Logan, Stoney, and PC Guthrie marched in. Then slowly drifted back to the TV.

The usual suspects were up there on the screen, pontificating as the ticker crawled along at the bottom of the picture. '"No": 1,402,047 – "Yes": 1,171,708'

Stoney had a quick look around. 'No sign of Hadden. Maybe he's been and gone?'

Guthrie pulled up his combat trousers. 'Might be in the bogs?'

Logan pointed. 'The pair of you go check.' Yes, it might look a bit odd, the two of them going in together, but this way they were likely to make it out again alive.

As they marched off, Logan wandered up to the bar. 'Two tins of Irn-Bru, and one Diet Coke. Don't need glasses.'

The barman sighed, then turned and took them out of the fridge. Placed them in front of Logan. 'You vote today?'

'Yup.' He pulled out the photo Stoney had downloaded. 'You seen this guy?'

A pause. Then a raised eyebrow. 'World porridge champion?'

'Has he been in?'

'Don't remember.' The barman turned and picked up a tumbler. Pressed it against an optic of Bells. Placed the whisky in front of Logan, along with the tins. 'That one's on the house for participating in the democratic process.' Delivered without a hint of a smile.

OK...

Logan paid for the other drinks and carried the lot over to the same table he'd had last time. Back to the wall. Good view of the rest of the bar and the entrance.

Two minutes later, Stoney and Guthrie emerged from the toilets and joined him.

'What took you so long?'

Guthrie twisted a finger through an imaginary lock of hair. 'Doing our makeup and talking about boys.'

Stoney shifted in his seat, having another look around. Then cracked the tab on his Diet Coke. 'Don't look now, but six o'clock. That not Kurt Murison?'

50

'Where?' Guthrie turned right around and stared.

Stoney hit him. Dropped his voice to a harsh whisper. 'I said, don't look!'

'How am I supposed to know if it's him if I don't look?'

Logan scanned the interior. Six o'clock. Even sitting down the man towered over the table. Broad shoulders. Shaven head. Ears that looked as if they'd been designed for someone a third the size. Huge hands.

He looked up and for a moment their eyes met.

Not romantic.

Logan glanced up at the television instead. Kept his voice low. 'Yup, that's Kurt Murison.'

'Crap.' Deep breath. 'What do we do?'

'Nothing. We sit here and we drink our fizzy juice and we wait for Alec Hadden to turn up.' He had a sip of Irn-Bru. 'And if Kurt makes a move, the two of you follow him and arrest him.'

Guthrie pulled a face. 'You sure? Because I remember what happened the last time someone tried it. DS MacEachran was in traction for six weeks.'

'DS MacEachran is an idiot.'

'True.'

They sat. And they waited. And they drank their fizzy juice.

Up on the TV, someone in an ill-fitting suit was going on about the new political landscape and how great it was everyone had come out to play.

Stoney checked his watch. 'What if Hadden's a no show?'

'Then you and Guthrie still get to arrest Kurt Murison.'

'Oh joy.'

The ticker ran the latest scores again. '"Yes": 54.47% "No": 45.53%'

'You know what?' Stoney turned his Diet Coke round in a circle. 'Maybe it's for the best? I mean, if we'd got

51

independence, we'd just be swapping one load of shiftless thieving useless bastards for another lot, wouldn't we?'

Guthrie sniffed. 'Yeah, but they'd be *our* shiftless thieving useless bastards.'

Logan polished off the last of his Irn-Bru, 'And, to be fair, we're already paying for two lots of them... Uh-oh – we've got movement.'

Kurt Murison scraped back his chair and got to his feet. Dear God, he was even bigger standing up. His arms were too big to hang loose at his sides, instead they stood out from his huge chest, as if he was carrying an invisible barrel under each one. He turned and lumbered towards the toilets, leaving a half-empty pint and an open packet of crisps behind. Safe in the knowledge that no one would *dare* touch them.

Guthrie pushed his tin away. 'Probably off to coil a Douglas, or, perchance, a Thora.'

'Don't be daft.' Stoney rolled his eyes. 'Tell him, Guv: men do Douglases, women do Thoras. Basic biology, isn't it?' He peered over his shoulder. 'Maybe we should go after him? Catch him with his pants down.'

Logan shook his head. 'We're police officers, Detective Constable Stone, not monsters.'

That got him a sigh. 'You know what I think?' Stoney dunked a finger off the tabletop. 'I think Scotland, England, Ireland, and Wales should all get their own parliament, and then once a week they do this big joint videoconference to decide stuff that affects everyone. That way we could fire half the buggers and save ourselves a fortune.'

Guthrie shook his head. 'Better idea: performance-related beatings for all politicians. Could put it on TV and charge people to phone in with suggestions.' He had a half-arsed attempt at a Geordie accent. 'It's day two in the Westminster house, and the Prime Minister's trying to weasel his way out of a kick in the nads.'

52

Stoney mimed picking up the phone, joining in with an OTT Cockney. 'Cor blimey guvnor, Oi'm gonna bid fifteen quid to see him battered wiv an *'addock*!'

'And here's the leader of the opposition, still dressed in a rubber gimp suit after making a prick of himself on Monday.'

'Luv a duck! Twenny quid if ye paddle his arse wiv an electric *saaaaaandar*.'

Guthrie grinned. 'See? You could wipe out the deficit in a single season.'

'This is genius, we should call Channel Four.'

Logan leaned back in his seat and left them to it.

Still no sign of Alec Hadden. Assuming, of course that Elaine hadn't made it all up in the first place. Maybe Chris Browning *was* one her regulars? Still, why would she lie about being paid to slander him? What was in it for her? Didn't make any... Hold on.

The front door barely creaked, as a thin man slipped in. Had to be a regular, because no one looked up from their drink. Shoulder-length brown hair, pointy chin. This year's World Porridge Champion. Alec Hadden.

So Elaine wasn't lying after all. Wonders would never cease.

Hadden had a quick peer about, then made for the bar. Stood there with his back hunched, in conversation with the bartender. Got himself a pint of Export.

Stoney and Guthrie had extended their brief to take in the United Nations and nipple clamps. Logan leaned forward and hushed them. 'Alec Hadden. At the bar. Right now.'

Guthrie slipped a hand into his pocket and pulled out the cuffs. 'You want to grab him straight away, or let him settle in?'

'Ah...' Stoney licked his lips. 'Might be an idea to get it over with while Kurt's in the toilet? He sees us slapping the cuffs on someone, it'll kick off.'

True.

'OK.' Logan pushed back his chair. 'Let's go see what Mr Hadden has to say for—'

The front door banged open and the whole bar did its *Deliverance* impersonation again. Silence. Stare.

Then Logan groaned.

Sodding DCI Sodding Steel. She stood in the doorway, wobbling slightly. One eye screwed shut, the other roving the place.

'Oh *great*.'

She lurched across to the bar and dug a hand in her pocket. Came out with a handful of change and a few notes. Clacked them down on the bartop. A couple of pound coins rolled off along the front of the taps. 'Grouse. Make it a … a brace.' She grabbed onto the wood with one hand, keeping herself upright.

The barman nodded. 'Double Grouse, coming right up, *Chief Inspector*.' Raising his voice on that last bit, just to make sure everyone heard.

Over at the next table, a large woman with a tattoo of seagulls flying around her thick neck rolled her eyes. 'Not more sodding cops. Like a bloody masonic lodge in here tonight.'

Steel took her drink and wacked it back in one go. 'Again.'

Then she turned, new drink in hand, and squinted around the room. Wobbled in place. Pointed up at the TV where a bloke in a suit stood before a big display banner with views of Aberdeenshire on it. 'Shhhhhh…! Turn it up, turn it up.'

The barman sighed, then did.

'… *turnout is eighty-seven point two percent. The total number of votes cast for each answer to the referendum question in this area are as follows. "Yes": seventy-one thousand, three hundred and thirty-seven. "No": one hundred and eight thousand, six hundred and six.*'

A roaring cheer erupted from the telly.

And when it had died down, *'I'm not quite finished.'*

Laughter.

Steel clenched one fist, the other wrapped around her glass, and bellowed up at the TV. 'YOU BUNCH OF UTTER BASTARDS!' Whisky slopped onto the wooden floor.

The barman cranked the sound down again.

Everybody stared at her.

The bathroom door clunked shut again, and there was Kurt Murison, wiping his hands on his jeans. 'Who's bastards?' His voice was unusually high for someone who looked as if they could eat rusty nails.

Stoney closed his eyes and swore. 'It's going to kick off, isn't it?'

Kurt loomed over Steel. 'Come on then. Who's bastards?'

She twirled round, more whisky joining the spillage. 'Aberdeenshire. All of them: *bastards*.' She jabbed her free hand at the screen. 'Look at it! Over sixty percent "No".'

A shrug. 'Their prerogative, isn't it? Democracy and that. Will of the people.'

'The people are dicks.' She raised the glass to her mouth and swigged, but there wasn't a lot left. 'Oh...' She clunked it down on the bar. 'Again.'

'Got to respect the outcome, don't matter what side you voted. All still Scotland.'

'They can respect my sharny arse.' She rocked a little, then frowned up at him. 'Here, do I know you?'

Hadden inched away down the bar. Putting a bit of space between himself and the coming storm.

Kurt jabbed a thick, meaty finger into Steel's shoulder. 'People like you make me sick, with your "Remember Bannockburn" and quotes from sodding *Braveheart*.'

Guthrie got to his feet and pulled out the CS gas to go with his handcuffs. 'Here we go.'

Steel poked Kurt back. 'What's wrong with that?'

'I don't remember Bannockburn, 'cos I wasn't sodding there. And neither were you. We forgived the Germans for bombing Clydebank flat – that was only seventy-three years ago – and you're holding a grudge from Thirteen Fourteen!'

Her eyes narrowed, then widened. 'I know you! Kurt "The Mangler" Murison. You've got warrants out on you.'

He flexed his shoulders. Loomed some more. 'Who's asking?'

Stoney swore again. Stared at Logan with a pained expression. 'Tell Sonja I loved her...' Then he got out his CS gas and stood shoulder to shoulder with Guthrie. Put a bit of steel in his voice. 'Alright, that's enough.'

Everyone in the place turned to stare at him.

He cleared his throat. 'Kurt Murison, I'm detaining you under Section...'

But Kurt didn't explode. Instead he turned and legged it, battering out through the pub's double doors.

Guthrie grinned. 'Yeah, you better run!'

Logan thumped him. 'Don't just stand there, you idiot, get after him!'

'Right.' And they were off, the pair of them charging after Kurt, CS gas and handcuffs at the ready.

8

Steel grabbed hold of the bar again. Burped. 'Was it something I said?'

Everyone else went back to their drinks as Logan walked over to the bar. 'You're a disaster, you know that, don't you?'

'Maybe it's my perfume?'

Alec Hadden had eased himself closer to the door. Another five feet and he'd be gone.

Logan grabbed a handful of his collar. 'Oh no you don't.'

Hadden bit his bottom lip. Didn't struggle. 'Sod.'

'Think you and I need to have a little chat, don't we, Alec? Maybe you can share your world-beating porridge recipe?' He dragged the thin man back to the table. Pushed him down in to a seat. 'You want to make this easy, or difficult? I'm happy either way.'

Thin fingers drifted across the tabletop. 'I don't know what you're talking about. Maybe you've got me mistaken for—'

'Chris Browning.'

'Ah...' He stared down at his wandering fingers. 'Right.'

Steel lurched up to the table and thunked three large whiskies down. Rocked in her chair. 'What we talking about?'

'Mr Hadden is about to tell me why he paid two prostitutes to lie about Chris Browning being a regular. Weren't you Mr Hadden?'

Silence.

'Or would you like to do this down the station?'

He shrugged one shoulder, curling into it until his ear was pinned against his jacket. 'It was ... you know ... to counteract the lies?'

'The lies.'

'For months, that puffed-up frog-faced git's been on the telly and the radio and in the papers, giving it doom and gloom, yeah? We're going to have no jobs. No currency. No defence budget. All the big companies are going to leave us. Won't be able to pay our benefits, or pensions, or doctors. Got kinda ... fed up of it.' His shrug swapped sides. 'Thought it'd even the scales a bit if everyone thought he liked getting it rough from a pair of hoors.'

Logan stared at him. 'And that passes for grownup political debate where you come from, does it?'

Steel threw her head back and laughed. A proper full-throated roar that set everything jiggling. 'You wee dancer.' Then she slapped Hadden on the back and pushed one of the whiskies in his direction. 'You earned it.'

He pulled on a lopsided smile. 'Thanks.' Then a sigh. 'Didn't help though, did it?'

She gave his shoulder a shoogle. 'Cheer up. Always next time. None of this once-in-a-generation bollocks, we've got what...' She turned and blinked at the TV for a bit. 'Laz?'

'Forty-five percent.'

'See? Forty-five percent. All we need's for one person in twenty to change their minds, and it's fifty-fifty!'

The smile grew a bit. 'Supoose.'

'Damn right.' She held up her glass. 'Slàinte mhath.'

Hadden clinked his drink against hers and they drank.

Logan took the glass off him. 'So you're saying you had nothing to do with Chris Browning going missing?'

'God, no. No, all I did was slip a couple of quid to Elaine and Jane. Told them to phone the *Examiner* and say Browning liked it rough and kinky. Honest. Ask them. And that wasn't till after he went missing.'

Logan just stared at him.

'*Honest*. I mean I know it was childish and that, but I wanted... It didn't seem fair they were always trying to scare people and ... it ... the "Yes" campaign needed... I...' Pink spread across his cheeks. 'Sorry.'

'You do know defamation is against the law, Mr Hadden?'

'Meh, it's civil, no' criminal.' Steel pushed Logan's free, untouched, thank-you-for-participating whisky across the table to Hadden. 'Our wee friend here wasn't trying to hurt anyone, was he? Just wobble the balance *our* way a bit.'

'Please. I'm really, really sorry.'

'There you go: he's sorry.' She knocked back her Famous Grouse. 'Didn't even work in the end.'

Their shoulders dipped.

Up on the TV screen, they called the Fife results. "No": 55.05%, "Yes": 44.95%.

Only one more local authority to declare and that was it.

Hadden gulped down the free whisky. Huffed out a breath. 'Look, can I ... I don't know ... buy you a drink or something? As an apology.'

Steel beamed. 'Course you can!'

Logan shook his head. 'Going to need you to come back to the station and make a statement.'

'Don't you listen to him, Haddy. You go get your Aunty Roberta a nice double Macallan and we'll say no more about it.'

'Thank you.' Hadden got up and went to the bar.

Logan watched him go. 'You do know he'll try to do a runner, don't you?'

But he didn't. He bought three whiskies and he brought them back to the table. Shared them out. 'I'm really, really sorry. I am. It was just ... I dunno, stupid.'

Steel helped herself to a double and wheeched it down. 'Ahh... Nice.' She pointed at Logan's. 'You're on duty, right?' Then helped herself to that one as well.

'Whoops...' Steel's legs didn't seem to be working any more. Probably due to the fact that they'd be knee-deep in whisky on the inside. 'M'fine...' Her smile spread and faded and spread and faded, as if it was out of focus. 'Cldn't be brrrrr.'

Half six in the morning and the bar crowd had thinned out again. Now, only the hardcore remained – clinging to their drinks in much the same way that Steel was clinging to the table. 'Whhhsssssssski.'

Hadden nodded towards the bar. 'Should I...?'

'No chance.' Logan stood. 'Whatever hangover she's got in the morning will be punishment enough.'

Steel peered up at him. 'Wanmorrrr.'

'Don't care. You're going home.'

'Awwwww...'

He dug his hands into her armpits, but it was like trying to pick up a pile of loose socks. Every time he got one bit upright, another bit collapsed.

Hadden hurried round to the other side. 'Let me give you a hand.'

Between them they wrestled her to her feet. Then caught her before she hit the ground. Turned and frogmarched her out through the front doors and onto Regent Quay.

The first hints of dawn curled pale blue at the corners of the sky, doing nothing to overpower the docks' spotlights.

Half six, and Aberdeen was waking up. The sound of traffic picking up on the dual carriageway.

Hadden shifted his grip on Steel's other arm. 'Where to?'

Closest place would be Logan's flat, but if she was going to puke she could sodding well do it somewhere else. Station, or her house? Hmm...

'Back to the station.' She could owe him one. And this way her wife wouldn't be left wading through a lake of pizza-and-whisky vomit.

'You got a car?'

'Nope. Walked.'

High overhead, a seagull screamed.

'Going to take a while then.' Hadden frowned. 'We could take my car? Got vinyl seat covers, in case she... You know.'

And Steel 'you know'-ing was very likely indeed. Plus, the sooner he could make her someone else's problem the better. 'Yeah, that'd be good, thanks.'

Hadden led the way with the left-hand side of Steel, while Logan followed with the right. She just dangled in the middle, making burbling noises.

'I'm really sorry about Chris Browning—'

'It's OK. Enough. I get it.' Logan puffed out a breath. 'You screwed up.'

'I know, but—'

'She was right, it's a civil law matter, not criminal. If Chris Browning wants to sue you for defamation when he turns up, that's his business. Hold your hand up and settle out of court. It'll cost you a lot less than paying for his lawyers *and* yours.'

A little smile. 'Thanks.'

They half-walked-half-carried Steel along the road, then left into James Street – another claustrophobic little alleyway that connected Regent Quay to the dual carriageway. Alec Hadden's rusty Volvo sat at the end, with most of its rear end sticking out over the double yellows.

Logan leaned Steel against the car's back door. 'Right, you'd better give me the keys.' He held his hand out to Hadden. 'You've been drinking.'

'Yes. Right. Of course.' He took out the keys, complete with little tartan fob, and passed them over. 'That's what I meant.'

'Good.' Logan plipped the locks open, and they wrestled her into the backseat.

'Erm...' Hadden pointed. 'Think we should put her in the recovery positon or something? Just in case?'

He had a point.

Logan rearranged her arms and legs, till it was as close as he could get given the space. She could barf away to her heart's content and not choke on the chunks. The footwell was going to end up in a hell of a mess, though. 'OK, let's get—'

Something hard battered into the back of his head, sending him sprawling, filling his skull with the sound of burning and the smell of broken glass...

A voice in the distance. 'Sorry.'

Then another thump and everything went—

9

Steel slumped back against the pillow and groaned. 'How could you do it? To *me*?'

'How could I?' Logan reached over and poked her in the shoulder. 'What about you?'

'Don't you even dare.' She clacked her lips open and closed a couple of times, then shuddered. 'Tastes like a badger threw up in my mouth...'

He looked around the room: embossed wallpaper painted a vile shade of pale pink. Polished floorboards with a knotted rug. Dresser in the corner with a mirror above it. Flatpack wardrobe. One window, and a door. And, of course, the bed. All shiny and brass with a barred headboard and foot-board, little sceptre things on the corner posts. 'Where are we?'

She puffed out her cheeks. 'Susan's going to kill me when she finds out.'

The view through the window was nothing but blue sky and clouds.

'What happened to our clothes?'

'I mean, bad enough cheating on her, but with a man? With *you*?'

'Will you shut up and focus? We didn't do this – Alec Bloody Hadden did.' Logan reached up with his spare hand and ran his fingers across the back of his skull. Winced as a hundred needles tore through his scalp. There was a lump back there that felt the size of a hardboiled egg, the hair spiky and stiff. Probably dried blood. 'Ow...'

She scowled at him. 'Who the hell is Alec Hadden?'

'He was the scumbag buying you whisky last night.'

The expression on her face didn't change.

'The Regents Arms? Remember? You staggered in half-cut and tried to pick a fight with Kurt Murison?'

Steel curled her top lip. 'Kurt "The Mangler" Murison? God, I *must* have been drunk.'

'Had to carry you to the car. Then sodding Alec Hadden battered me over the back of the head.' And when Logan got his hands on him, he'd repay the favour with a stiff boot in the testicles. Hadden was going to come down with a bad case of resisting arrest. There was a second bump, beside the first. More needles. 'Ow...'

'Well stop poking at it then!' She raised her head from the pillow and grimaced. 'Look at it: pink! No' even a nice pink – *Barbie* pink. Who paints a bedroom Barbie pink? What are they, six?' A sniff. 'Where's my clothes?'

'How would I know?' He nodded to himself. 'Right, we need to get out of here.'

'*Really*? Gosh, whatever made you think of that? You must be some sort of genius!'

'Shut up and think. How do we get out of the cuffs?'

'Don't look at me. Only time I've ever been handcuffed to a bed there's been spanking and safewords.'

'Yeah, thanks. That's a *lot* of help.' Logan stared at the end of the bed, where their feet poked out from under the duvet. His right ankle was shackled to the bars, but Steel's weren't. 'Why didn't he cuff your legs too?'

She pulled her feet in, hiding them. 'Got a verruca. Maybe he's squeamish?'

'That, or you're too short and your legs don't reach.'

'I am no' short! Perfectly normal size for a Scottish woman.'

'Keep telling yourself that.' Logan stuck his free leg out of the bed and put his foot on the floor. Pushed. Nothing happened. A second time, harder this time, and the bed frame creaked, then shifted half an inch to the right. Big brass bed with two fully grown adults in it – of course it was going to be a sod to shift. Especially with only one leg.

'Hoy!' Steel hit him. 'Stop shoogling about. Sodding handcuff keeps digging into my wrist.'

Again. Gritting his teeth and shoving.

'Ow! What did I just tell you?'

He stopped and stared at her. 'I'm trying to move the bed, that OK with you?'

'No' if I end up with a broken wrist, it isn't.'

'God's sake… Fine.' He took hold of her hand, lacing the fingers together. 'Happy now? This way it won't tug at your *delicate* skin.' Logan dug his heel in and pushed.

She peered over the edge of the bed. 'What *exactly* are you trying to achieve?'

'If we can get to the wardrobe, there'll be clothes. That OK with you?'

Another shove. Another half inch. And already the muscle in his thigh was shouting at him. One more shove and it was screaming.

'Going to take all sodding week at this rate.' She stared at the window. 'What time do you think it is?'

'How should I know…' A final push and he slumped back, panting, leg dangling. Just going to have to take it in stages. They'd probably moved about as far as a fun-sized Mars Bar.

'Supposed to be back on shift at five.'

'Good for you.' He dug his heel in and pushed again.

'Someone's going to notice we're missing.'

If anything it was getting harder. 'Come on you wee sod...' Maybe the rug was bunching up under the bed's legs?

'And then they'll come running. Batter the door down. Barge in here with their...' She slapped a hand over her eyes. 'Nooooo. They'll see me in the nip. In bed. With *you*.'

'How? How will they even know where we are? You were half-cut to start with. They'll think you're just hungover and copping a sicky.'

'I *am* hungover.'

'And whose fault is that?'

'Oh shut up.'

'You shut up.'

Another push. More panting. One more ... and cramp tightened like a fist around his calf, twisting the muscle into a burning knot trying to rip its way free of the bone. 'Aaaaaagh.'

'Oh for God's sake. Stop it.' Steel thumped her other hand against his chest. 'Not getting anywhere.'

The pain tightened again. He had to force the words out between clenched teeth. 'Well I don't see *you* doing anything.'

She stared at the ceiling. 'Fine.' Then a deep breath. 'Close your eyes. And keep them closed till I tell you. Because if you even *think* of peeking...'

'Why would I want to peek? Bad enough imagining it, never mind seeing it for real!'

'Close your sodding eyes!'

He did, and the duvet shifted as Steel slipped out of the bed. He grabbed hold of his half and held on tight before it slipped and everything was on show.

Her feet made a soft slapping sound as they hit the floor. 'Stark, bare-arsed naked and handcuffed to a man. Never been so embarrassed in my *life*.'

Then there was some grunting. Some swearing. And finally

the bedframe shifted, moaning in time to Steel's heaves. Groan. Squeal. Groan. Squeal. Groan—

A clunk from the other side of the room and a man's voice. 'What...?'

Logan's eyes snapped open.

Alec Hadden stood in the doorway, mouth hanging open, a newspaper tucked under one arm and a bottle of water in the other.

'Aagh!' Then Steel leapt back into bed, burrowing under the duvet as if her life depended on it. But not quick enough to protect Logan from an eyeful.

He shuddered. Oh God...

Her cold skin slapped against his leg, then she recoiled to the edge of the bed, taking as much of the duvet with her as possible.

Logan held on for grim death.

She let go of his hand.

'What are you doing?' Alec stepped into the room. Closed the door behind him.

Steel stuck her head above the covers. 'WHERE THE HELL ARE MY CLOTHES?'

'Ah.' He settled down on the edge of the bed, shoulders drooped, head bowed. 'They're in the wash. You were sick, like, *everywhere*. I mean on the car seat, in the footwell, on yourself, on your friend here. Everywhere.' A shrug. 'So I bunged everything in the washing machine.'

'YOU SAW ME NAKED!'

'Only for a little bit.' A sigh. Then he took out the newspaper and held it up. The headline 'UNION BACK' sat over a big union jack flag. A shocked Salmond in one corner, a smug looking Cameron in the other. Alec gave another big, theatrical sigh. 'Forty-five percent "Yes", fifty-five percent "No", and they're calling it a *decisive* victory. How? How is that decisive? Yeah, it's a *decision*, but that's all it is.'

Steel jabbed a finger in his direction. 'You just abducted two police officers, sunshine. You think that's a good idea?'

'Now they're talking about backing out of all that Devo-Max stuff they promised. It's rash. It was unwise. England won't let Scotland have anything if they don't get what they want first.'

'Listen up, chuckles: you're no' getting away with this. They'll already be out there looking for us. How long do you think it's going to take them to kick in your door, eh?'

'They lied to the Scottish people. They laid out this bowl full of promises: more power, more influence, more money, and now Westminster wants to take it all back.'

Logan shuffled as far up the bed as he could. Which wasn't far with the handcuff fastening his right leg to the frame. 'Politicians lie, Alec. It's what they do. Not exactly a shocker, is it?'

'We could have been free...'

'I know it's disappointing, but it's the way it is. This is what democracy looks like. You just have to accept it, put it behind you, and move on.'

He turned and stared out of the window. 'Why should we? Why shouldn't we arm ourselves and take back our country? Referendum didn't work. It's time for revolution.'

Steel grabbed a pillow and battered it off Alec's head. 'Don't be so sodding wet.'

'Don't—'

'Unlock these handcuffs, *now*.'

'You'll arrest me.'

She looked at Logan. Then at Alec, eyebrows up. 'Of course we'll sodding arrest you! What did you think was going to happen? You abduct two police officers, you strip them, and you chain them to the bloody bed, did you think we'd bake you a cake?'

Logan held up his other hand. 'OK, OK, let's all calm

down. No one's starting a revolution, and no one's arresting anyone.' He pointed at the handcuffs around his ankle. 'Alec, can you unlock them, please? They're cutting off circulation to my foot.'

'I don't understand why everything went wrong.' He dropped the paper on the bed. Ran a hand through his long brown hair. 'I didn't want any of this. I just wanted...' His bottom lip trembled. 'I didn't mean to hit you. I just ... I panicked. I didn't...'

Steel rolled her eyes. 'Oh in the name of the wee man. Don't be such a big girl's blouse.' She shook her fist, making the handcuffs rattle against the brass bars of the headboard. 'Unlock these things and we'll talk about maybe getting you into a nice low-security prison.'

Alec licked his lips. Opened his mouth...

Whatever he was about to say, it was stopped by the sound of a doorbell somewhere on a lower floor.

Alec stood. 'I have to go.'

'Unlock these sodding handcuffs!'

But Alec didn't. Instead he stood. Chucked the paper onto the duvet. 'In case you get bored.' Then he grabbed Logan's side of the bed and dragged the thing back into the middle of the room. 'Don't move it again. You're scratching the floorboards.' He turned and marched out, closing the door behind him. The thump was followed by the *click* of a key turning in its lock.

Logan thumped back into his pillow. Then winced as the lumps on the back of his head got squished. 'Oh very clever. That was a spectacular bit of hostage negotiation, that was.'

'Kiss my—'

'You don't threaten the person you're negotiating with! Yeah, let us free so we can arrest you.'

'Of course we're going to arrest him.'

'You don't have to tell *him* that!'

'Close your eyes.' She grabbed his hand again, then slipped out from beneath the duvet. There was grunting, creaking, and swearing again as the bed moved. But they weren't going towards the wardrobe this time, they were going in the direction the bed was pointing.

'What are you doing?'

'I said no sodding looking!'

'I'm not looking.'

More grunts. More creaks. More swearing. Then *clunk*. Then the mattress springs twanged as Steel climbed back on the bed. 'Keep them closed!'

'Then tell me what the hell's going on.'

'Looking out the window… Down there. Can just see past a bit of roof, there's a car parked at the kerb.'

'Thrilling.'

'Shut up. Want to see who's visiting.'

'Open the window and shout for help.'

'Hold on…' Thump. Bang. A growling noise. Then, 'Open you wee sod…' More straining noises. 'Gah. It's locked. We… It's Rennie! And DC Stone. You wee dancers!' She banged on the window. 'BUGGERLUGS, UP HERE! HOY! UP HERE! LOOK UP YOU PAIR OF MORONS!'

'What are they doing?'

'NO! DON'T GO BACK TO THE CAR! WE'RE UP HERE! HOY! RENNIE YOU SODDING IDIOT!'

Silence.

'What?'

A long, rattling sigh, and then Steel collapsed back on the bed beside him. 'They drove off.'

'Oh, that's just *brilliant*.'

'We're going to be stuck here for ever, aren't we?'

10

Logan stared up at the ceiling as Steel climbed under the duvet again. 'How could they just drive off?'

'Because they're idiots.' She groaned. Covered her face with her free hand. 'No' that this situation isn't dramatic enough, but it's about to get worse.'

'What now?'

'I need a pee.'

Breath whooshed out of him. 'You are *not* peeing the bed.'

'I'm peeing in, or on, something, whether you like it or not.'

'Well... pee in the wardrobe then. Or better yet: tie a knot in it. You don't...'

She frowned at him. 'How am I supposed to "tie a knot" in it? Have you no idea how a woman's body—'

'Shhh...'

Logan stared at the door.

Click.

It swung open, and there was Alec Hadden back again. With a length of chain in one hand and a padlock in the other. His mouth tightened and his eyes widened. 'What did I tell you about moving the bed? You've scratched the hell out of the floor! Look at it. LOOK AT IT!'

'Think it's bad now?' Steel sniffed. 'Wait till I pee on it.'

He dropped the chain and the padlock. 'You horrible… How…' He clenched a fist. Took a deep breath. Nodded. 'I see. What we have here is a lack of respect.' Alec unbuckled his belt.

Steel stuck her chin out. 'If you think you're putting your dick anywhere near me, you've got another think coming!'

He pulled his belt from his trousers. Curled one hand around the buckle, and wrapped the leather around his fist a couple of times, leaving the end dangling. 'I didn't want to do this. You made me.'

'You sodding *dare*!'

Logan held his hand up again. 'Come on, we all need to calm down here. This isn't going to solve anything. We…'

Alec lunged, swinging the belt overarm at Steel, teeth bared.

She dodged to the side, grabbed the belt and yanked him towards her. Then slammed her forehead into his face.

There was a wet crunch and he went sprawling across the bed. Steel was up on her knees, everything airing in the breeze – pale, swinging, and wobbling – as she hammered her fist down into Alec's head. Once. Twice. Three times. He struggled up, and she mashed her fist into the bloody mess of his nose.

Thunk.

Alec wobbled. Rocked. Then his eyes crossed and he slid backwards off the bed. Thump onto the floor. Lying spread-eagled on the scarred floorboards. Not moving.

Steel let out a shuddery breath. 'God, now I *really* need to pee.'

'So search him again.' Steel pulled the duvet up beneath her chin. Her free hand was swollen and curled, the skin darkening from red to purple. Probably broke something.

Logan heaved Alec over onto his back again. It was cumbersome and awkward, but nothing compared with the effort of hauling him up onto the bed in the first place. 'It's not here.'

'Then where the hell is it?'

'I don't know, do I? Maybe he didn't keep the handcuff key on him? They're not his handcuffs, they're ours. Maybe he doesn't even know what the handcuff key *looks* like?'

'Oh this is just great. Thank you very much.'

'How is this my fault? You're the one who battered him.'

'What was I supposed to do?'

Lying on the bed, Alec groaned. His face was a mess – swollen and bloodied, a couple of teeth missing. Most of his nose wasn't where it was supposed to be any more.

'He's waking up.'

Steel sooked a breath through her teeth. 'You hit him this time. My hand hurts.'

Logan rolled him into the middle of the bed, getting scarlet smears on the duvet cover, and stuck his free leg out. Reaching with his toes for the dropped chain. Holding his breath and stretching for it. The handcuff dug into his other ankle. 'Got it.'

He wrapped his toes around the cold metal and pulled it, clinking back to the bed. Reached down and grabbed the end.

Steel looked over his chest at the floor. 'What about the padlock?'

'Give us a chance...' His foot reached, and reached, and reached. Logan's tongue poked out the side of his mouth.

But there was no way he could even come close.

'You need to push the bed closer so I can reach.'

'For goodness sake. Do I have to do everything?'

'Yes. You have to do everything. I'm contributing absolutely *nothing* here.'

'You're such a whinge. Close—'

'I know. Close my eyes.' He shuddered. 'Trust me, some sights I never want to see again.'

'Oh: ha, ha.' She slipped out and the bed groaned and creaked and gouged its way across the floorboards. 'This ... was ... easier ... when ... there was ... just ... your fat ... arse on ... there.' The bed came to a halt and Steel climbed beneath the duvet again. 'Right, you can open your eyes.'

He grabbed the padlock with his toes and together they chained Alec's hands behind his back. Then wrapped the rest of it around his ankles, before pulling it tight and padlocking the two ends together. Leaving him trussed up like a turkey.

Steel put her foot on his shoulder and shoved him over the edge of the bed.

Alec tumbled to the floor with a thump and a groan.

'Serves you right.' She wriggled down into the bed and scowled up at the ceiling.

'What now?

'Still need a pee.'

'Wardrobe?'

A sigh. 'Wardrobe.'

'What do you mean there's no clothes in there?'

Steel's voice came out muffled. 'I mean, there's hundreds of clothes. Millions of them. It's like a branch of Markies in here. What do you think I mean?'

'Wonderful.'

'Hey, I'm not enjoying it much either...' A pause. 'Urgh. I've got pee on my feet!'

'I spy, with my little eye, something beginning with "B".'

Lying next to him, Steel sniffed. 'Better no' be "boobs". You promised no' to peek!'

'It's not "Boobs". And one glimpse was enough to scar me for life, thanks.'

'Blinds?'

'No.'

'Don't stop!' Steel gripped his hand, the cuffs digging into his wrist as the bed moaned and creaked beneath them. 'Harder!'

Logan grunted and put his hips into it as the whole frame swayed and clanged.

'Come on, come on, come on...'

'Argh...' He slumped back against the mattress, sweat prickling between his shoulder blades. 'It's no good.'

'We can *do* this!'

'No we can't. The frame's not going to fall apart. Doesn't matter how much we shoogle it.'

'Sodding hell.'

'Because I'm thirsty, OK?' Logan wriggled as far as to the left as the cuffs around his wrist and ankle would let him, right hand groping at the floorboards. 'Little more...'

'Sodding hell.' Steel grunted and groaned, and the bed gouged its way across the floorboards again.

'Come to Logan...' The bottle of water Alec dropped was just out of reach.

More grunts and groans.

'Got you!'

'OK...' Steel frowned at the ceiling. 'Shoot Gordon Brown, shag Nick Clegg, marry David Cameron.'

Logan raised an eyebrow. 'You'd marry a Tory?'

'He's worth millions, isn't he? Soon as we're married, there's going to be an unfortunate accident and I'll inherit the lot.' A grin. 'An unfortunate accident with a wood chipper. Hello Daveyboy, I've made you a lovely cup of tea. Come out into the garden and drink it next to this dirty big chunk of machinery. Whoops! Shove. Grrrrrrrrrrrrrrrrrrind!'

'Urgh.' She curled her top lip. 'Your hand's all sweaty.'

'So stop holding it, then.'

'Can't. Every time I let go you shoogle about and I get a chafed wrist. You're like a ferret in a carrier bag. A sweaty ferret. That can't hold still for two minutes.'

'This is hell, isn't it? I've died and I've gone to hell...'

'I'm bursting, OK?' Logan crossed his legs. Didn't help though, was still like a spaniel dancing on his bladder.

Steel pulled a face. 'Serves you right for drinking all that water.'

'I was thirsty.'

'So go pee in the wardrobe.'

'How?' He levelled his voice, weighed out each word as if talking to a very small, very stupid child. 'My ankle's handcuffed to the *bed*. I can't get *off* the bed like you can. If I *could* we wouldn't be in this sodding mess.'

'You're a dick, you know that, don't you?'

'Going to have to pee off the edge of the bed.'

'Oh great. So I widdle in the wardrobe like a civilised human being, and you just pish all over the floor like some sort of animal. And then we get to lie here marinating in the stench.'

He turned and stared at her. 'You don't exactly piddle rosewater yourself.' Then he jerked his head at the corner of the room. 'Shove the bed over there and I'll pee in the corner. Well, corner-ish.'

'Oh God, I can hear it splashing!'

'Will you shut up? This isn't exactly a precision instrument at the best of times.'

'Urgh...'

'Something beginning with "D"?' Logan glanced around the room. 'Door?'

'Nope.'

'Dresser.'

76

'Nope.'

Hmm... Ah, of course – dangling from the side of the blinds. 'Drawstring.'

'Nah. Give up? It's him on the floor: "Dickhead".'

The little creases deepened between Steel's eyebrows. 'It's just, sometimes, I really miss my dad, you know? He'd have loved Jasmine.'

'He OK with the whole gay thing?'

'Course he was. What's not to like?'

'Fair enough.' Logan frowned up at the ceiling, making patterns from the light and shadow. 'Never really knew my father.'

'Oh aye, Mum put it about a bit, did she?'

A laugh barked out of Logan, setting the mattress vibrating. 'Can you imagine?' Then a shudder. 'Actually, better not. No, he was in the Job. Constable Charles McRae. Went to pick up a bloke on a warrant for aggravated burglary in Stonehaven. Only the guy had a sawn-off shotgun and wasn't cool with going back to prison again. I was five.'

Steel reached across the duvet with her spare hand and gave his shoulder a squeeze. 'Sorry.'

'Why do you think I joined the force? Couldn't think of anything that would hack my mother off more.'

'Pfff... Curtains?'

Logan shook his head. 'Nope.'

'Carpet?'

'That's not a carpet, it's a rug.'

'Oh.' She chewed at her top lip. 'Cushions?'

'Give up?' He pointed at the window. 'Clouds.'

'What? It has to be *inside* the room, you idiot. Who taught you how to play?'

*　　*　　*

'Oh-ho, Chuckles is on the move.'

Logan peered over the edge of the bed. Steel was right: Alec Hadden was twitching. Then a groan. Then a cough that left a smear of red-flecked sputum on the floorboards.

Steel raised her eyebrows. 'Thought I'd killed him for a bit there.'

A tremble ran through Alec, wrists and ankles still firmly chained and padlocked behind his back. 'Gnnnnnnngh...' And then he went limp again.

'Serves you right, you wee shite. That's what you get for abducting police officers.'

11

'Well?'

Logan's fingers walked along the bedframe, tracing the corner where the headboard joined the main frame. Smooth metal, slick and cool. There – a hexagonal lump. 'It's a nut.'

'So undo it!'

He grabbed the sides and twisted.

Nothing.

Tried again. Gritted his teeth. 'Come on you wee sod...' Fire raced through his fingers, up into his palm. Then wrist. Then, 'It won't budge. Too tight.'

'Right. So we need to loosen it. OK.' She sucked at her teeth. 'Don't have a spanner, just have to go back to shoogling. Clockwise shoogling.' A breath. 'Come on Roberta, you can do this.' She poked Logan in the shoulder. 'Eyes. And *keep* them closed.'

He scrunched them shut. 'OK.'

She folded the duvet back on top of him, then there was some grunting.

The handcuff around his wrist twisted. 'Ow, ow, ow, ow!'

'You think that's bad?' Her weight settled on top of him, one knee on either side. 'How do you think I feel?'

He slapped his hand over his eyes as well, just in case.

'I swear Laz, if you get a stiffy during this—'

'Just get on with it.'

'Deep breath, Roberta. Think of Natalie Portman.' Then the thrusting started. Back and forward. Harder. Making the frame creak. Then Steel added a side-to-side thrust of the hips, getting the bed to make little circles. Harder and faster.

Logan pulled his head further into the pillow, out of the way of anything that might be swinging about up there.

Creaks, groans, pinging noises, grunting.

This would be a *really* bad time to be rescued.

Ping, creak, groan, grunt, then thumping joined the mix. Probably the bed's legs banging on the scarred, piddled-on floorboards. Her voice was laboured, squeezed out between breaths as she kept on grinding. 'Try now!'

Oh God. Don't look. Don't look.

He slipped his hand back beneath the bed, feeling for the nut.

The whole thing rocked and wobbled, joints opening up and closing with each thrust. Be lucky if he didn't lose a finger.

The nut was cold and hard in his hand. Logan grabbed it. Squeezed. Twisted… 'Come on!'

And it gave. Not much, but a tiny twist. Again. As long as he timed his turn with the right point in the rotation the nut loosened. Again. And again. And again. 'It's coming! Yes! It's coming!'

Then it wasn't coming any more. The nut jolted out of his grasp and the whole side of the bed collapsed as he snatched his hand out of the way.

'You wee beauty!'

'Ow…' If anything it was even more uncomfortable than being handcuffed to the unbroken bed. Now the whole frame was out of alignment and the cuff around his wrist and ankle were pulling him apart.

Steel scrambled off him. 'Keep those sodding eyes shut.' Then there was more grunting and groaning. But thankfully no thrusting. 'Come on... Agggggghhhhhh... Break you wee—'

Clang.

And the other side of the bed collapsed too.

'Woo-hoo!'

The scuff of bare feet on floorboards. Then she let go of his hand. 'Right, I need you to sit up.'

Logan did as he was told, struggling in the darkness, dragging the headboard with him.

'Keep going. Forwards. Grab your ankles.'

'This better not be more kinky stuff.'

'Just do it.' Then another bout of grunting as the headboard shifted. 'Going to wedge the bars over the corner post... There you go. Might want to grit your teeth for this bit.'

'What? What are you— Aaaaagh!' Pain ripped through his wrist as the handcuffs tried to bend it in a way it really hadn't evolved for.

'One more go.' A grunt.

'Are you *trying* to kill me?'

Then a *ping* rang out and the pressure on his wrist disappeared.

Logan risked a peek. She'd used the corner post as a lever to snap one end of the bar out of place. And now the handcuffs were free. He shut his eyes again before he saw anything else.

'HAHAHAHAHAHAHA! I'm a sodding *genius*!' Steel slapped him on the back. 'Told you I'd get us out of here. Now we do the same crowbar trick with the footboard, and we're good to go. Brace yourself.'

Groan. Strain. *Ping.*

Logan slid backwards down the mattress.

They were free. Naked and still handcuffed together, but at least they weren't attached to that bloody bed any more.

'OK, you can look now.' Steel stood and raised her free hand like the Statue of Liberty. The duvet cover was wrapped around her in a makeshift toga. 'Tres stylish, nes pa?'

'I feel like a complete dick.' Two floral pillowcases, tied together, didn't make a great loincloth, but it was better than nothing.

'Look on the bright side – I can't see yours, so we're good to go.' She paused to nudge Alec Hadden with her foot. 'We'll be back for you, Chuckles. Don't get too comfy.'

As if that was possible, lying on a wooden floor, trussed up with chains.

Logan led the way over to the door, the other handcuff dangling from his ankle – scrapping along the boards.

'Hoy!' Steel hit him. 'What did I tell you about shoogling and these sodding cuffs?'

He closed his eyes. Counted to three. 'Fine.' Then took her hand again. 'OK?'

She looked down at their hands, then up at his naked torso, then down at his makeshift loincloth and the pale, pasty legs poking out underneath it. 'Don't think George Clooney's got much to worry about.'

Why bother?

He opened the door. Peered out. A stairway reached down two storeys, new looking, with magnolia walls and framed prints of wildflowers. That would make this an attic conversion then. Another doorway opened off the small landing on a room crowded with boxes.

Steel sniffed. 'What if there's another one of him?'

'Think they might *just* have heard us destroying the bed.'

Down the stairs, carpet soft and warm underfoot. A

window looked out on the back garden. A whirly washing line sat in the middle of a square of green, heavy with clothes. *Their* clothes. Getting dark out there, the sky heading from clear blue to navy.

First floor. Three white-panelled doors led off the landing.

'Shhh!' Steel stopped, head cocked to one side as something growled. 'Starving.' She pointed downstairs. 'Kitchen – food. Then out the back door and get our sodding clothes.'

'Think you can keep your stomach in check for five minutes while we get dressed? Not that much to ask, is it?'

'Hungry.' She straightened her toga. 'And in case you're wondering: Detective Chief Inspector still outranks Detective Sergeant.'

'Detective *Inspector*.'

'Acting Detective Inspectors don't count.' She took a step down the stairs, hauling him with her. 'You want to play with the big girls? Get a proper promotion.'

God's sake...

He followed her down to the ground floor. Didn't really have any option with his wrist still cuffed to hers. Holding hands as if they were on some sort of horrible, deviant date.

The kitchen lay at the end of the hallway – a pristine expanse of shiny tiles, stainless steel, and polished-wooden work surfaces.

Steel made straight for the fridge. 'Sandwich would do... Oh.' Her shoulders drooped. 'All they've got is a carton of fake butter and an onion. And that doesn't look too fresh.'

Logan stretched out an arm and opened the bread bin. Pulled out a loaf of sliced white and dumped it on the counter next to the toaster. Stuck a couple of slices in and pushed down the handle. 'OK? You happy now?'

She sniffed. 'Think if you're going to abduct someone, the least you could do is get a bit of cheese in. Some smoked ham. Few eggs.' Steel grabbed the butter and clunked the fridge shut again. Tried one of the cupboards. 'Pot Noodle would do at a push.'

Steel chomped on her toast, melted buttery spread glistening on her chin. 'Hurry it up, going full-on football studs here.'

Gloom enveloped the back garden. Two small patches of light spilled out through the kitchen window and the open back door, just enough to make their breath shine in the cool evening air.

Logan unpegged his pants from the whirly. 'Close your eyes.'

Steel raised an eyebrow. 'In this cold? It'll be all shrivelled up like a half-chewed fruit pastille anyway. Get a move on.'

He hauled them on, then took his trousers off the line and pulled them on too. Then ditched the Laura Ashley loincloth. The shirt was more of a challenge – could only get it on over one arm, buttoning it up across his chest as far as possible, the other sleeve hanging limp at his side. Same with the jacket.

Steel popped the last chunk of toast in her mouth, then sooked her fingers clean. 'Where's mine?'

'You were eating.'

'Make with the bras and pants, you unchivalrous wee sod.'

He passed her the underwear, trying *really* hard not to see how red and lacy it was. Then stood there, cheeks like barbecues, as she struggled into both. Shifting around, hand-cuffed wrist twisting so she could fasten her bra behind her back.

Don't touch her bare skin, don't touch her bare— Agh ... too late.

The figures reflected in the kitchen window looked like something from a Cohen Brothers movie. Steel with her random hair – fully suited, except for the one bare arm and shoulder – Logan her taller, slightly less scruffy, mirror image.

She scowled, then scratched at her naked armpit – where the rogue bra strap dangled. 'Off-the-shoulder's no' a good look for you. No' with those pasty arms.'

'How am I supposed to know what he's done with our keys?'

'Still,' she shrugged, 'on the bright side: there's no risk of you flashing your horrible man bits any more. Thank heaven for tiny wrinkly mercies.'

'Yes, because you're Keira Knightley meets Marilyn Monroe, aren't you?' He tightened his grip on her hand and pulled her through into a utility room, just off the kitchen. It smelled of warm laundry. The contents of their pockets were piled up on the work surface above the washing machine: phones, keys, cash, wallets, warrant cards, and all the other bits and bobs. 'Yes!' He grabbed the keys and flicked through them. 'No.'

She peered at the silvery collection in his hand. 'No what?'

'No handcuff key.'

'Must be. Give.' She did exactly the same thing that he had. With exactly the same result. 'Bugger.'

'I told you, didn't I? Honestly.'

'Blah, blah, blah.' She picked her e-cigarette from the pile of stuff and clicked it on. Sooked hard on the mouthpiece. Closed her eyes and sighed. 'Ooooh, God, that's better...'

Logan powered up his phone. 'I'll give Stoney a ring and—'

A thump came from somewhere above.

They both looked up at the ceiling.

Steel curled her free hand into a fist. 'If that wee scumbag's wriggled free, he's getting a flying lesson out the nearest window.' She dragged Logan back into the kitchen, then out into the hall.

His left thumb skiffed across the screen, never hitting the right button. 'Would you slow down?'

'No.' Up the stairs to the first landing.

'How am I supposed to—'

'Shhh...' She put a finger to her lips. 'Listen.'

Another thump. Not overhead this time, but off to the left.

She pointed at one of the three doors. Mouthed the words, 'Three. Two. One.' Then a nod.

Logan grabbed the handle and twisted. Threw the door open. 'POLICE! NOBODY... Oh.'

It was a single bedroom. And there was a man on the bed. Well, not so much 'on' as 'chained to' by the arms and legs. Naked except for an adult nappy, with a ball gag in his mouth. Middle-aged, pasty skin, with receding brown hair, wide sunken eyes, and a stubbly beard.

Steel pursed her lips and raised an eyebrow. 'Aye, aye, someone's been naughty.'

He writhed on the bed, mumbling behind the ball gag.

Logan hauled her over to the bed. Then glanced down at his own half-on-half-off clothing. 'I know it doesn't look like it, but we're police officers. I'm going to unbuckle the gag, OK?' He reached forward, pulling Steel's arm with him, and fiddled with the buckle.

'Gaaaah!' Red weals cut across his cheeks, where the leather strap had been. He coughed a couple of times, then spat. Hauled in a breath. 'Oh God, you have to get help! Please! He'll be back soon!'

Logan frowned down at him. Take away the beard and... 'It's Chris Browning, isn't it? We've been looking for you for *weeks*.'

'*Guv? Hello?*' Stoney's voice came through the locked door. His silhouette rippled through the patterned glass on either side. Probably trying to see into the house. *'Hello?'* Then he knocked. *'Guv, you there?'*

Steel squatted down and levered up the letterbox flap. 'Give me your handcuff keys.'

'Guv? Can you unlock the door?'

'You deaf or something, Constable Stone? Keys, now.'

He stepped back. *'Someone's there with you, aren't they Guv? Are you being coerced? Stand back, I'm breaking the door down!'*

Logan slammed his free hand into the glass at the side, setting it booming. 'Just post your sodding keys through the letterbox!'

'But—'

Steel poked her hand through the nylon brushes. 'Give me the keys, or I'm going to reach down your throat, grab your pants, and haul them back out through your gob!'

The second ambulance pulled away from the kerb, lights spinning in the sunset. Steel pulled her e-cigarette from her pocket, clicked it on, and took a deep drag. 'Ahhh. That's better.'

Logan rubbed at the thick red line encircling his right wrist. 'There you go, we just saved an influential "No" campaigner.'

She shrugged. 'Win some, lose some.' She sniffed, then spat into the neat front garden. 'Anyone asks, the naked thing didn't happen. Understand?'

Goose pimples raced up Logan's arms, coming together at the back of his neck. 'Ack... I'm probably going to need therapy.'

'Official report, we were handcuffed to a radiator or something. No naked. No bed. No piddling.'

'Agreed.'

She turned and stared up at the building. 'So, come on then – how did you vote?'

'None of your damned business, that's how.' He lifted his chin and walked toward the waiting patrol car. 'Now, if you'll excuse me, I'm off to get very, *very* drunk.'

She shambled along beside him. 'Good idea.' Then reached out and took his hand again. 'You're getting the first round in, though.'

And however bad the hangover was, they'd just have to deal with it tomorrow.

Read on for an extract from the new
Logan McRae thriller,

The Missing and the Dead . . .

Run.

1

Faster. Sharp leaves whip past her ears, skeletal bushes and shrubs snatch at her ankles as she lurches into the next garden, breath trailing in her wake. Bare feet burning through the crisp, frozen grass.

He's getting louder, shouting and crashing and swearing through hedges in the gloom behind her. Getting closer.

Oh God...

She scrambles over a tall wooden fence, dislodging a flurry of frost. There's a sharp ripping sound and the hem of her summer dress leaves a chunk of itself behind. The sandpit rushes up to meet her, knocking the breath from her lungs.

Please...

Not like this...

Not flat on her back in a stranger's garden.

Above her, the sky fades from dirty grey to dark, filthy, orange. Tiny winks of light forge across it – a plane on its way south. The sound of a radio wafts out from an open kitchen window somewhere. The smoky smear of a roaring log fire. A small child screaming that it's not tired yet.

Up!

She scrambles to her feet and out onto the slippery crunch

of frozen lawn, her shoes lost many gardens back. Tights laddered and torn, painted toenails on grubby feet. Breath searing her lungs, making a wall of fog around her head.

Run.

Straight across to the opposite side as the back door opens and a man comes out, cup of tea in one hand. Mouth hanging open. 'Hoy! What do you think you're—'

She doesn't stop. Bends almost in half and charges into the thick leylandii hedge. The jagged green scrapes at her cheeks. A sharp pain slashes across her calf.

RUN!

If He catches her, that's it. He'll drag her back to the dark. Lock her away from the sun and the world and the people who love her. Make her *suffer*.

She bursts out the other side.

A woman squats in the middle of the lawn next to a border terrier. She's wearing a blue plastic bag on her hand like a glove, hovering it over a mound of steaming brown. Her eyes snap wide, eyebrows up. Staring. 'Oh my God, are you...?'

His voice bellows out across the twilight. 'COME BACK HERE!'

Don't stop. Never stop. Don't let him catch up.

Not now.

Not after all she's been through.

It's not fair.

She takes a deep breath and runs.

'God's sake...' Logan shoved his way out of a thick wad of hedge into another big garden and staggered to a halt. Spat out bitter shreds of green that tasted like pine disinfectant.

A woman caught in the act of poop-scooping stared up at him.

94

He dragged out his Airwave handset and pointed it at her. 'Which way?'

The hand wrapped in the carrier bag came up and trembled towards the neighbour's fence.

Brilliant...

'Thanks.' Logan pressed the button and ran for it. 'Tell Biohazard Bob to get the car round to Hillview Drive, it's...' He scrambled onto the roof of a wee plastic bike-shed thing, shoes skidding on the frosty plastic. From there to the top of a narrow brick wall. Squinted out over a patchwork of darkened gardens and ones bathed in the glow of house lights. 'It's the junction with Hillview Terrace.'

Detective Chief Inspector Steel's smoky voice rasped out of the handset's speaker. *'How have you no' caught the wee sod yet?'*

'Don't start. It's... Woah.' A wobble. Both hands out, windmilling. Then frozen, bent forward over an eight-foot drop into a patch of Brussels sprouts.

'What have I told you about screwing this up?'

Blah, blah, blah.

The gardens stretched away in front, behind, and to the right – backing onto the next road over. No sign of her. 'Where the hell are you?'

There – forcing her way through a copse of rowan and ash, making for the hedge on the other side. Two more gardens and she'd be out on the road.

Right.

Logan hit the send button again. 'I need you to—' His left shoe parted company with the wall. 'AAAAAAAARGH!' Cracking through dark green spears, sending little green bombs flying, and thumping into the frozen earth below. THUMP. 'Officer down!'

'Laz? Jesus, what the hell's...' Steel's voice faded for a second. *'You! I want an armed response unit and an ambulance round to—'*

'Gah...' He scrabbled upright, bits of squashed Brussels sprouts sticking to his dirt-smeared suit. 'Officer back up again!'

'Are you taking the—'

The handset went in his pocket again and he sprinted for the fence. Clambered over it as Steel's foul-mouthed complaints crackled away to themselves.

Across the next garden in a dozen strides, onto a box hedge then up over another slab of brick.

She was struggling with a wall of rosebushes, their thorned snaking branches digging into her blue summer dress, slicing ribbons of blood from her arms and legs. Blonde hair caught in the spines.

'YOU! STOP RIGHT THERE!'

'Please no, please no, please no...'

Logan dropped into the garden.

She wrenched herself free and disappeared towards the last house on the road, leaving her scalp behind... No, not a scalp – a *wig*.

He sprinted. Jumped. Almost cleared the bush. Crashed through the privet on the other side, head first. Tumbled.

On his feet.

There!

He rugby-tackled her by the gate, his shoulder slamming into the small of her back, sending them both crunching onto the gravel. Sharp stones dug into his knees and side. The smell of dust and cat scratched into the air.

And she SCREAMED. No words, just a high-pitched bellow, face scarlet, spittle flying, eyes like chunks of granite. Stubble visible through the pancake makeup that covered her thorn-torn cheeks. Breath a sour cloud of grey in the cold air. Hands curled into fists, battering against Logan's chest and arms.

A fist flashed at Logan's face and he grabbed it. 'Cut it out! I'm detaining you under—'

'KILL YOU!' The other hand wrapped itself around his throat and squeezed. Nails digging into his skin, sharp and stinging.

Sod that. Logan snapped his head back, then whipped it forward. *Crack* – right into the bridge of her nose.

A grunt and she let go, beads of blood spattering against his cheek. Warm and wet.

He snatched at her wrist, pulled till the hand was folded forward at ninety degrees, and leaned on the joint.

The struggling stopped, replaced by a sucking hiss of pain. Adam's apple bobbing. Scarlet dripping across her lips. 'Let me go, you *bastard*!' Not a woman's voice at all, getting deeper with every word. 'I didn't do anything!'

Logan hauled out his cuffs and snapped them on the twisted wrist, using the whole thing as a lever against the strained joint.

'Where's Stephen Bisset?'

'HELP! RAPE!'

More pressure. 'I'm not asking you again – where is he?'

'Aaaaagh... You're breaking my wrist!... Please, I don't—'

One more push.

'OK! OK! God...' A deep breath through gritted, blood-stained, teeth. Then a grin. 'He's dying. All on his own, in the dark. He's *dying*. And there's nothing you can do about it.'

2

The windscreen wipers squealed and groaned their way across the glass, clearing the dusting of tiny white flakes. The council hadn't taken the Christmas decorations down yet: snowmen, and holly sprigs, and bells, and reindeer, and Santas shone bright against the darkness.

Ten days ago and the whole place would have been heaving – Hogmanay, like a hundred Friday nights all squished into one – but now it was deserted. Everyone would be huddled up at home, nursing Christmas overdrafts and longing for payday.

The pool car's wheels hissed through the slush. No traffic – the only other vehicles were parked at the side of the road, being slowly bleached by the falling snow.

Logan turned in his seat and scowled into the back of the car as they made the turn onto the North Deeside Road. 'Last chance, Graham.'

Graham Stirling sat hunched forwards, hands cuffed in front of him now, dabbing at his blood-crusted nostrils with grubby fingers. Voice thick and flat. 'You broke my nose...'

Sitting next to him, Biohazard Bob sniffed. 'Aye, and you didn't even say thank you, did you?' The single thick eyebrow that lurked above his eyes made a hairy V-shape. He leaned in, so close one of his big sticky-out ears brushed Stirling's forehead. 'Now answer the question: where's Stephen Bisset?'

'I need to go to hospital.'

'You need a stiff kicking is what you need.' Biohazard curled a hand into a hairy fist. 'Now tell us where Bisset is, or so help me God, I'm going to—'

'Detective Sergeant Marshall! *Enough*.' Logan bared his teeth. 'We don't assault prisoners in police cars.'

Biohazard sat back in his seat. Lowered his fist. 'Aye, it makes a mess of the upholstery. Rennie: find somewhere quiet to park. Somewhere dark.'

DS Rennie pulled the car to a halt at the pedestrian crossing, tip-tapping his fingers on the steering wheel as a pair of well-dressed men staggered across the road. Arms wrapped around each other's shoulders. Singing an old Rod Stewart tune. Oblivious as the snow got heavier.

Their suits looked a lot more expensive than Rennie's. Their haircuts too – his stuck up in a blond mop above his pink-cheeked face, neck disappearing into a shirt collar two sizes too big for it. Like a wee boy playing dress-up in his dad's clothes. He glanced over his shoulder. 'You want the court to know you cooperated, don't you, Graham? That you helped? Might save you a couple of years inside?'

Silence.

Stirling picked a clot of blood from the skin beneath his nose and wiped it on the tattered fabric of his dress.

'The DI's serious, Graham, he's not going to ask you again. Why not do yourself a favour and tell him what he needs to know?'

A pause. Then Stirling looked up. Smiled. 'OK.'

Biohazard pulled out an Airwave handset. ''Bout time. Come on then – address?'

His pink tongue emerged, slid its way around pale lips. 'No.

You and the boy have to get out. I talk to him,' pointing at Logan, 'or we go back to the station and you get me a lawyer.'

'Don't be stupid, Stirling, we're not—'

'No comment.'

Logan sighed. 'This is idiotic, it's—'

'You heard me: no comment. They get out, or you get me a lawyer.'

Rennie's face pinched. 'Guv?'

'No comment.'

Logan rubbed his eyes. 'Out. Both of you.'

'Guv, I don't think that's—'

'I know. Now: out.'

Rennie stared at Biohazard.

Pause.

Biohazard shrugged. Then climbed out onto the empty pavement.

A beat later, Rennie killed the engine and followed him. 'Still think this is a bad idea.'

Clunk, the door shut, leaving Logan and Graham Stirling alone in the car.

'Talk.'

'The forest on the Slug Road. There's a track off into the trees, you need a key for the gate. An ... an old forestry worker's shack hidden away in there, *miles* from anywhere.' The smile grew hazy, the eyes too, as if he was reliving something. 'If you're lucky, Steve might still be alive.'

Logan took out his handset. 'Right. We'll—'

'You'll never find it without me. It's not on any maps. Can't even see it on Google Earth.' Stirling leaned forward. 'Search all you like: by the time you find him, Steve Bisset will be long dead.'

The pool car's headlights cast long jagged shadows between the trees, its warning strobes glittering blue-and-white against the needles. Catching the thick flakes of snow and making them shine, caught in their slow-motion dance to the forest floor.

Logan shifted his footing on the frozen, rutted track. Ran his torch along the treeline.

Middle of nowhere.

He wiped a drip from the end of his nose. 'Well, what was I supposed to do? Let him no-comment till Stephen Bisset dies?'

The track snaked off further into the darkness, bordered on both sides by tussocks of grass, slowly disappearing under the falling snow, glowing in the torchlight.

On the other end of the phone, Steel groaned. *'Could you no' have let the nasty wee sod fall down the stairs a few times? We're no' allowed to—'*

'You want to tell Stephen's family we let him freeze to death, all alone, in a shack in the forest, because we were more concerned with following procedure than saving his life?'

'Laz, it's no' that simple, we—'

'Because if that's what you want, tell me now and we'll head back to HQ. You can help Dr Simms pick out a body-bag. Probably still got some nice Christmas paper knocking about, you could use that. Wrap his corpse up with a bow on top.'

'Will you shut up and—'

'Maybe something with kittens and teddy bears on it, so Bisset's kids won't mind so much?'

Silence.

'Hello?'

'All right, all right. But he better be alive. And another thing—'

He hung up and marched over to the pool car.

Biohazard leaned against the bonnet, arms folded, shoulders hunched, one cowboy boot up on the bumper. Nose going bright red, the tips of his taxi-door ears too. He spat.

Nodded at the ill-fitting suit behind the steering wheel. 'The wee loon's right, this is daft.'

'Yeah, well, I've cleared it with the boss, so we're doing it.'

A sniff. 'What if Danny the Drag Queen tries it on when you're out there?'

Logan peered around Biohazard's shoulder.

Stirling was slumped in the rear seat, blood dried to a black mask that hid the lower half of his face. Bruises already darkening the skin beneath both eyes. The blue sundress all mud-stained and tatty after the chase through the gardens. Shivering.

'Think I'll risk it.' Logan pulled out the canister of CS gas from his jacket pocket, ran his thumbnail across the join between the safety cap and the body. 'But just in case, get his hands cuffed behind him. And I want the pair of you ready to charge in.'

Logan popped open the back door and leaned into the car. It smelled of sweat and fear and rusting meat. 'Out.'

Twigs snapped beneath his feet as they picked their way between the grey-brown branches, following the circle of light cast by Logan's torch. A tiny dot, adrift on an ocean of darkness.

Something *moved* out there. Little scampering feet and claws that skittered away into the night.

Logan flicked the torch in its direction. 'How much further?'

He jerked his chin to the left. 'That way.' The words plumed out from his mouth in a glowing cloud, caught in the torchlight. Curling away into the night. Dragon's breath.

Down a slope, into a depression lined with brambles and the curled remains of long-dead ferns, already sagging under the weight of snow. More falling from the sickly dark sky.

Stirling's feet clumped about in Rennie's shoes, the scuffed black brogues and white socks looking huge beneath the torn sundress and laddered tights.

Up the other side, through the ferns – brittle foliage wrapping around Logan's trousers, leaving cold wet fingerprints. 'Why him? Why Stephen Bisset?'

'Why?' A shrug. The torchlight glinted off the handcuffs' metal bars, secured behind his back, fingers laced together as if they were taking a casual stroll along the beach. 'Why not?' A small sigh. 'Because he was *there*.'

Logan checked his watch. Fifteen minutes. Another five, and that was it: call this charade off. Call in a dog team. Get the helicopter up from Strathclyde with a thermal-imaging camera. Assuming Steel could pull enough rank to get them to fly this far north on a Friday night in January.

They stumbled on between the silent trees. Fallen pine needles made ochre drifts between the snaking roots, the branches too thick to let the snow through.

He stopped, pulled up his sleeve – exposing his watch again. 'Time's up. I'm not sodding about here any longer.' He grabbed the plastic bar in the middle of the handcuffs and dragged Stirling to a halt. 'This is a waste of time, isn't it? You're never going to show me where Stephen Bisset is. You want him dead so he can't testify against you.'

Stirling turned. Stared at Logan. Face lit from beneath by the torch, like someone telling a campfire horror story. Tilted his head to the left. 'You see?'

Logan stepped away. Swung the torch's beam in an arc across the trees, raking the needle-strewn forest floor with darting shadows…

A sagging wooden structure lurked between the trunks, in a space that barely counted as a clearing, partially hidden by a wall of skeletal brambles.

Stirling's voice dropped to a serrated-edged whisper. 'He's in there.'

Another step. Then stop.

Logan turned. Shone the torch right in Stirling's face, making him flinch and shy back, eyes clamped shut. Then took out his handcuff key. 'On your knees.'

A thick stainless-steel padlock secured the shack's door. It had four numerical tumblers built into the base, its hasp connecting a pair of heavy metal plates – one fixed to the door, the other to the surround. Both set up so the screw heads were inaccessible.

Logan flicked the torch beam towards Stirling. 'Combination?'

He was still on his knees, both arms wrapped around the tree trunk, as if he was giving it a hug. Hands cuffed together on the other side. Cheek pressed hard against the bark. 'One, seven, zero, seven.'

The dials were stiff, awkward, but they turned after a bit of fiddling. Squeaking against Logan's blue-nitrile-gloved fingertips. Clicking as they lined up into the right order. The hasp popped open and he slipped the padlock free of the metal plates. Slipped it into an evidence bag.

Pushed the door.

Almost as stiff as the padlock wheels, it creaked open and the stench of dirty bodies and blood and piss and shite collapsed over Logan. Making him step back.

Deep breath.

He stepped over the threshold. 'Stephen? Stephen Bisset? It's OK, you're safe now; it's the police.'

Bloody hell – it was actually colder *inside* the shack.

The torch picked out a stack of poles and saws and chains. Then a heap of logs and an old tarpaulin. Then a cast-iron stove missing its door. Then a pile of filthy blankets.

'Stephen? Hello?'

Logan reached out and picked one of the poles from the stack. Smooth and shiny from countless hands over countless years. A bill hook rattled on the end, the screws all loose and rusted. 'Stephen? I've come to take you home.'

He slipped the hook under the nearest blanket and lifted. Oh Christ…

Outside. The cold air clawed at the sweat peppering his face. Deep breath.

Logan rested his forehead against a tree, bark rough against his skin. The smell of pine nowhere near strong enough to wash away the shack's corrupt stench.

Don't be sick.

Be professional.

Oh God…

Deep breath.

'I…' His throat closed, strangling the words. Pressed his forehead into the bark so hard it stung. Tried again. 'I should kick the living shit out of you.'

Stirling's voice oozed out from the darkness. 'He's beautiful, isn't he?'

The phone trembled in Logan's hands as he dug it out and called Steel. 'I've found Stephen Bisset.'

There was a whoop from the other end. Then, *'Laz, I could French you. Is he…?'*

'No.' Though if he ever woke up, he'd probably wish he was. 'I need an ambulance, and an SEB goon-squad, and a Crime Scene Manager, and someone to stop me stringing Graham Bloody Stirling up from the nearest tree.'

KILLER READS

DISCOVER THE BEST IN CRIME AND THRILLER.

SIGN UP TO OUR NEWSLETTER FOR YOUR CHANCE TO WIN A FREE BOOK EVERY MONTH.

FIND OUT MORE AT
WWW.KILLERREADS.COM/NEWSLETTER

Want more? Get to know the team behind the books, hear from our authors, find out about new crime and thriller books and lots more by following us on social media:

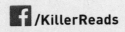 /KillerReads   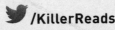 /KillerReads